The *Jump*

Freya Johnson

Dedicated to; Ms. Rossum,
For believing in me, and sharing amazing
memories with me this last year.

And to Stephenie and Alyson; For inspiring me,
and allowing my young author dreams
to come true from your own worlds and characters.
Thank you.

"Don't cry because it's over,
Smile because it happened,"
-Dr. Suess

One

You never think about a loved one dying until it's too late. You realize you haven't spent as much time as you'd wished with them, and after they pass you wish you had more time. More time to make memories, more time to be with them, and more time to love them. The same thing was going through my mind, as I saw the love of my life jump off a cliff, trying to save my life.

"His name was Felix White," The news reporters started the next morning. "The last person he was seen with was his supposed girlfriend, Carmen Brooks," I cringed at the *supposed* she added to my title. "If *anyone* has any more information, please call-"

Dad turned off the sound of the television, and looked over at my sad self, wrapped up in a blanket Felix gifted me for our one-year anniversary last year, with tear-stained cheeks from crying all night. He didn't say anything, he just looked sorry for me for having to hear about Felix all over the news and having hundreds of DMs online from strangers asking about how I was.

Francis and Alice, Felix's parents, sent over most of his things, including shirts, CDs, records, books, and blankets. They also gave me his journal, which they skimmed over and thought it'd be better to give to me since it had lots of pages and songs he wrote about me.

They also offered to bring over the piano he had, but there was no room for it in our small, 2 bedroom 2 bathroom home. My parents allowed me to stay home for the next week, or however long I needed, to clear my head on what I'd seen, and what had happened. My friends, Jenny, Alex, Harley, and Michael, had offered to come over and try to cheer me up, but we all knew I needed some alone time.

I slugged upstairs to my room, which had Felix's blankets, pillows, and the one other matching cat stuffed animal we had gotten on our first date. I collapsed onto my bed and started crying. The feeling of my boyfriend's name, and face, along with mine, being all over the news of our town, was too much for me. Along with the few people who made a theory that I was fed up with Felix, and *pushed him off a cliff.*

Dad had gone to the store yesterday after I came home in tears, water, and blood. He got my favorite snacks and drinks and picked up Felix's stuff while my mother washed me up and comforted me. Even with the amount of comforting my parents were doing, it wasn't enough to fill the hole in my heart that made me want to jump off a cliff myself. Somehow, Alice had realized I was thinking like that, and sent me a note, telling me not to do that, and reminding me that the world wasn't over, and I was free to visit Felix's room and piano whenever I wanted.

I spent the majority of the days at home crying in my room and listening to Felix's favorite songs. Jenny and Michael tried to call me, but I sent them a text saying I wasn't in a good mood, and they understood.

Carly, Felix's sister, called me a couple of times, I answered and listened to her tell me how sorry she was, and that she wished there was something she could do. I told her it was okay and that these sorts of things happen, but she didn't believe me. She convinced me to go to an arcade. It was just us and her brother Josh. I won a big panda bear, and she won a lot of various prizes. She gave most of them to me, and I tried to decline but she said it was a gift, so I couldn't.

Josh was a tall, muscular man, who was about the same age as Felix. They were brothers, and Felix had only really told me about him a couple of times. But Josh, being the kind person he is, handed me a big cat plushy, the one other color that Felix and I didn't have. The cat was black, with a white spot around its eye, and I had the matching dark brown cat with a light brown spot, and Felix had the matching orange cat with a dark orange spot.

Carly and Josh took me home in their red Lamborghini, and people all over the street were staring at me, the girl in the passenger seat of a Lamborghini, smiling, laughing, and singing along to the songs on the radio, a week after her boyfriend had passed.

There was a 'fancy' knock at my door, and I automatically knew it was my mother, since she knocked 3 times, waited for an answer, and knocked again, calling my name.

"Carmen, you have a letter, it says it's from Felix. I don't know if it's something Francis and Alice found, but you might want to read it, honey."

"Mom…" I paused, sniffling, sitting up, and wiping the tears, and tiredness from my eyes. "Can you come in, please?" As soon as I said that, Mom was at my side, rubbing my back, and handed me the fancy, tan envelope, with my name printed in Francis' handwriting neatly on the front.

I opened the envelope and was met with a neatly folded letter that had a warning to "read while alone" on it. Mom saw and set a kiss on my forehead and excused herself, smiling hopefully as she closed the door fully, walking down the narrow hallway.

I slowly peeled back the note, turned the lamp on my left nightstand, and took a sip of water. The note read

Carmen,

I know you are upset and confused, but I just ask you not to cry over Felix's "disappearance". He is okay. I need you to come over as soon as possible and talk with me and Alice.

-Dr. Francis White.

That note changed my entire tone. I got up and rushed out to the living room. I grabbed my messenger bag and left out to my gray Honda Civic. I started the engine and reached to call Alice, but she called before I even unlocked my phone.

"You're on your way?" She asked, trying to get straight to the point.

"Yeah... how did you know?..." I asked, taken aback by her amazing sense of what I was about to do.

"I can explain to you when you get here, Carmen..." The voice stopped, and I heard shuffling and the phone passing to someone.

"Carmen, are you okay?" Francis asked, his slight British accent being a pleasurable sound.

"Yeah... can I know what's going on?" I pulled out of the drive and started slightly speeding down the road to the White's house.

"We will tell you as soon as you get here, we don't want to scare you off."

He chuckled slightly, as I heard a slight low murmur in the background. He responded to his laugh with;

"I must go now, see you soon. Goodbye, Carmen."

"Thank you, Francis" I answered just seconds before he ended the call. I pressed the CD button on my radio, and it started playing the CD Felix had put in here last.

I pulled into the White's driveway and walked up a couple of stairs to the big, rustic cottage they owned. They also lived in the middle of a forest, near a small lake of theirs. I was greeted by Carly at the front door.

"There is something we would like you to do before we explain anything to you." She explained, happily, with a grin on her face that spread from ear to ear. Carly was always the happy one, and I wonder how she manages that.

I remembered the first day of school when I had met Jenny, and she was introducing me to the Whites, explaining who they were. Carly was the one who was always happy. And Felix was the hot, music-listening, know-it-all. Carly's grin slightly decreased as she cringed, as if she heard my memory.

Francis directed me to Felix's room, telling me that I should get some sleep, obviously noticing that I haven't gotten much. I shuffled over to the room with the amazing scent, and closed the door, laying down on his pillow and blanket-covered neat bed in the middle of the room, with records, CDs, and books stacked up on the shelf built into the wall. I turned to the large carved-out spot and noticed his spare record player, in the spot his gold, polished one used to sit that was sitting on my desk at home. I turned on one of the many copies he had of his favorite artist and stared at the tall ceiling. I wished that I could be lying on the bed with him and his arms wrapped around me, as he hummed the tune of the song he composed for me.

I fell asleep thinking about him like I do every night, but this time was different. It wasn't sad, it was comforting and happy.

Two

I ended up falling asleep, lying in the same space I would have if he was lying there with me. I dreamt of what Francis and Alice would tell me when I awoke, and of Felix. His dirty blond hair and his amazing hazel eyes stared down at me and comforted me. I dreamt of the house we would live in, the college we would go to, and everything that we would do together for the rest of our lives.

When I awoke, Carly was sitting on the edge of the bed, and humming to the music that I had kept on for the entirety of the night

"You've been asleep for a couple hours, Carmen. I was told to make sure you weren't dead." She softly chuckled to herself and looked at me with her bright amber eyes. "Francis and Alice would like to speak with you after you call your parents and tell them you're alright. They think something bad happened to you." She zoomed out of the room before I could even ask how she knew that, but I think that was the point, she couldn't tell me yet.

I scrolled through my phone contacts and called Mom, she immediately answered, and asked a ton of questions, like "How are you?", "Are you okay?" and my personal favorite, "Did you get *kidnapped?*"

"No, Mom, I didn't get *kidnapped...* I'm alright, I just fell asleep in Felix's room, that's all."

"Okay good, because I've been trying to call for the last 2 hours, and your phone went straight to voicemail."

"Mom," I started, making my voice sound serious. "My phone was off and I was sleeping. I'm *okay*, there is *no* reason to worry."

"Be glad I didn't call the cops and make a scene" She muttered under her breath. I laughed and she tried to hide the smile I could hear in her voice, but it was as audible as could be.

"Okay, now that we've cleared I'm okay, and that you *don't* have to call the police, I'm going to go. I'll keep my phone on vibrate. I love you."

"Alright, stay safe, I love you, Carmen." She said right before I hung up, and swung my legs over the side of the bed to stand up. I walked out of Felix's big room and walked to the living room, being met with Francis and Alice on the couch, watching the fireplace.

"Ah, Hello Carmen," Alice explained formally. She smiled and cleared her throat, trying to wipe the formal tone in her voice. "Please, have a seat, we've got some coffee and tea going if you'd like some." Francis smiled from behind her as she still struggled to clear the formality in her voice.

"Excuse her, Carmen. She isn't used to talking to people outside of work." He laughed and Alice went over to the giant kitchen, grabbing two cups of coffee for me and Francis, and a cup of tea for herself.

"Alice, how did you know I wanted coffee?" I asked as she set the cup on the coffee table in front of where I was about to sit.

"Huh, I guess we should talk about that." She relaxed into Francis' arms, finally relaxing her voice, and talking to me as if I were her kid. "Well, do you want to start, Francis." It wasn't a question. She was basically telling Francis that he was better at explaining this than her.

"Carmen, we needed to tell you first of all, that Felix is *okay*, But he isn't in a hospital, nor is he hurt at all."

He paused, waiting for my reaction, or some sort of claim, but I didn't want to overreact. My heart pumped faster, and they seemed to notice, I guess just doctor instincts. I tried not to let it show by taking a sip of coffee.

"Felix is okay because…" He stalled, looking at Alice as she nodded. "...He's *immortal*." This was it, my mind was spiraling, my heart rate spiked immediately, and I almost spit out my coffee, but was careful to swallow and didn't care that I looked shocked beyond belief.

"W.. What?" I choked out, shocked, and confused. I understood that he was okay, which didn't make sense from a fall at that height. But it was weird that that thought of *immortality* didn't cross my mind at all.

Francis and Alice then went on to tell me that he was in Canada, explaining to the *'Immortal Leaders',* why he had a significant other that caused his face and name to be all over the news and internet. I didn't say anything after that, I knew that it was my fault for overreacting, and for sharing all that information, but I thought the love of my life was dead, what else was I gonna do?

"Carmen… we know you're confused, and have a lot to think over, so how about we let you process-"

"No. I need to hear it all now." I tried not to sound on the verge of tears.

"You sure?" Alice asked as Francis went to refill my coffee cup and I nodded. Alice didn't talk until he sat back down and then nestled into his arms.

"Yes, I'm sure." I took a sip of my coffee and looked at the fireplace, trying to control my thoughts.

"Okay, I feel as if we must get it out of the way. Carmen… Us immortals can *read minds*. And that's how I knew how you were reacting to Felix's 'death', and knew when you were about to call me." She paused, letting me absorb that new, big wave of information. "Your mind was shielded by someone. That's why he hasn't reached out to you. Because he didn't know if you were so overly sad you wouldn't listen to anyone, if you took your own life, or if you hadn't cared at all." Alice stopped, even though she had more to say.

I realized I was crying, and that my tears were probably the reason why she stopped talking. I wiped the tears from my eyes, and Francis flashed over to me, making me stand up, and wrapping his arms around my shoulders helping me stay stable.

"I'm bringing you to his room to lie down for a little bit." Francis insisted. As I tried to argue, my crying just got heavier and louder. Alice zoomed past us, turning the music on as she read my mind, noticing I wished he was here. She whispered something to Francis and went out of the room.

Francis set me down on the bed, sat by me, and put a hand on my forehead, checking my temperature. "Alice is going to grab you water, and some melatonin to try and help you sleep."

"I-I don't want to sleep. I want to see *him*"

"Can you please *try*, Carmen? For him?"

"F-Fine," I choked out. Alice came back with the water and melatonin. She handed me the melatonin gummies and set the water on the little modern side table Felix had.

"You get some sleep, okay?" Alice told me, smiling and rubbing my hand and leaving alongside Francis.

I fell asleep, and it seemed like forever until I gained consciousness again. "Hey, my love." I heard a low, soft voice say as it sent shivers down my spine.

"F-Felix?" I asked, scared, yet turning my head a little bit to look at my beautiful lover that lay next to me, rubbing little circles in my back.

"I wish I knew what you were thinking right now." He chuckled and stopped rubbing my back, he reached to bring a hand to my warm, red cheek.

I turned to face him and grabbed him by his shirt collar, and pushed my lips onto his as they molded together to fit perfectly.

"I. Thought. You. Were. Dead." I said, in between kisses, taking a breath after every word. He smiled against my lips and kissed me for a little bit longer, and then pulled away from me, laying his forehead to mine.

"I'm sorry, love. I noticed how sad you were after it happened, and because you didn't know, I couldn't just be okay after jumping from that high of a fall.

"It's okay, I'm just glad you're alive." I pressed my lips to his again, and he smiled, kissing back.

"Someone's eager," he breathed out. I pulled away as he shifted himself to hover over me. I rubbed circles on his stomach, feeling the abs he had.

"I missed you," I admitted, even though he knew that. He laughed quietly and started kissing my cheek and jaw. I had a little shiver down my spine as he disconnected our lips and laid down next to me.

"I know, love. And I'm sorry, I'm just glad you're okay."

"Speak for yourself," I murmured, snuggling into his arms, laying my head on his chest as he wrapped an arm around my waist.

We sat like that for a while. He hummed the tune of the song I was playing, and he rubbed his hand across my waist, trying to comfort me and let me absorb this moment before I would face Francis and Alice again.

A couple of tears streamed down my face, and Felix worried. He brought a hand up to my face and wiped the tears away.

"You okay?" I nodded, but he didn't believe that. "Tell me what you're thinking." He looked at me, and rubbed his thumb over my cheek, making me flush an even brighter red as he chuckled. "You're cute, you know that?"

"Yeah… but I was just thinking about how things are going to go when people believe you're dead."

"My love, we could just make a "news post" about me and that I was okay, and in the 'hospital' " He made air quotes, trying to reassure me that it would all be sorted through.

I didn't say a word after that, and I almost fell asleep to the sounds of his humming and the comforting feel of him rubbing my back. He stopped me from sleeping, as he told me we needed to go talk to Francis and Alice and get help for what we would do about his 'death'.

"Carmen, we need to go get this situated with Francis and Alice." He looked at me with apologetic eyes, because he knew I wanted to lay like this for eternity, and so did he, but we had to go talk to them and get me home before it was too late and my parents started calling the cops. I sat up, trying to get myself situated, as he sat up with me and noticed my shirt.

"Hey! You're wearing my *Queen* shirt, I was wondering where that went." He laughed, putting an arm around my waist and helping me stand up by lifting my body so I was the same height as him, and then set me on the ground.

"Yeah… I have a lot of your stuff at home if you want it back." I blushed. He just chuckled slightly and then told me *the plan* as he spun me around and danced to the melody he composed for me.

"Since I already know what Francis and Alice are thinking, I'll tell you the plan. You're going to go home and tell your parents Francis is offering a 1 bedroom 2 bathroom cottage around Fairbanks, it's a small town near that college you wanted to go to. It's also very pretty." He added, pausing to make sure I was keeping up. "You're going to reassure them that this is *your decision*. As long as you tell them that, you're golden. The only thing they are worried about is the fact that you are going to be 'living alone', but we don't have to worry about that if you tell them about what happened. They are also going to ask about me because they read the letter Francis sent."

"Francis sent them a letter?"

"Yeah, they sent a letter telling them I'm in the hospital. You're going to tell them that I'm okay and that I'm just healing up. We need to say that I'm in a hospital outside of how far she is willing to drive..." He thought for a second. "The Bartlett Regional Hospital. It's in Juneau, and that's hours away from here." He paused, trying to listen to more of *the plan*. But he said the only thoughts in Francis and Alice's heads were that they were waiting for him to stop speeding through the details, and let them explain.

We went out to the living room, and Alice got up to get coffee, sensing I wanted some after just waking up, and some… red punch? For her, Francis and Felix.

"Alice… What is *that*?" I nodded towards the red container of juice she was putting back in the drinks fridge.

"Oh, I suppose we didn't tell you... That drink is what keeps us immortal." She said it casually like she was reading a book or something.

"But don't get any ideas." Francis added, reading the questions in my head like *"What would happen if I drank some?"* and *"Could I sneak some into my coffee?"* Even though it was obvious I wouldn't be able to, since they could read my mind, and run around at the speed of light. Francis chuckled at that remark of mine, settling down as he realized those thoughts were just my impulsive thoughts talking, and that I wasn't planning on doing anything with the suspicious red drink.

"Carmen, why don't you take a seat?" Francis suggested as Alice handed Felix and me our drinks. Felix pulled me by my waist to sit by him, and I was startled but eventually relaxed into his arms as he set his arm around my shoulders. "So we know that Felix shared some of *the plan* with you. Do you need a recap or are you alright if we pick up where he left off?"

"Uhm... I guess you could just continue, I'm sure I'll have to be reminded like ten more times anyways." I cleared my throat.

"Alright, give me just one second." He turned his head to look down at Alice, who was leaning against him and just looked at her. I wasn't too sure what he was doing. Felix chuckled, and looked over at me, smiling.

Three

"Give them a second," Felix whispered and laughed into my ear, "They thought it'd be rude to whisper, so they ended up telepathically talking to each other." Francis and Alice looked over at us and cleared their throats.

"I apologize, we didn't want to seem rude, but then came off as creepy." Francis smiled, trying to move on as I smiled back. "So Felix told you that tomorrow you would go home, and tell your parents that you were gone for so long because you had to visit Felix at the hospital. Only tell them the information they *need* to know, if they ask the hospital, tell them, if they don't ask the hospital, don't tell them." Francis paused and I nodded.

"I think she knows that, dear. Tell her the stuff Felix didn't." Alice grinned, looking up at Francis.

"Alright. Tell them about the 1 bedroom 2 bathroom cottage in Fairbanks that I'm offering to you guys. It *is* a house you guys can move into after Felix is "better." But you'll tell them that you're going to slowly bring stuff over every time you go to "visit Felix", and are going to get everything small enough to bring there in bags, hopefully before he is "fully healed" and can help you move the bigger things in a moving van together."

"What if they don't believe or trust me?" I looked up at Felix, as he squeezed my hand reassuringly.

"Then you'll have to *make* them believe. You can tell them that we are willing to talk to them, and then we can have a discussion, on our side, and theirs." Francis smiled, reading my mind as I was calming myself down, and eventually, everyone was smiling. Everyone but me. I was anxious, trying not to let it show. But apparently, I'm bad at that, because even Felix, the one person who *couldn't* read my mind, knew I was super worried and slightly scared.

"You'll be fine, love. There is no reason to worry." Felix whispered in my ear as I blushed.

"Okay, Felix will have to stay here, unless you want to act as if I dropped you off. Then you and Felix could say your goodbyes and such before you have to talk to your parents." Francis added, looking at me, waiting for my answer.

"Yeah, I think we should do that." I looked up at Felix as he smiled and placed a kiss on my forehead.

"Let's go then, Carmen." Felix stood up, his arm still wrapped around my waist so he took me up with him.

"Thank you Francis, and thank you, Alice. I'm so unbelievably happy to get this opportunity, and I'm super glad you told me. I won't be telling anyone anything. Thank you again." I didn't even recognize my voice, I sounded way too formal.

"Seth, Knock that off," Alice said, and she sensed I was confused at why she said that. "Oh, right. We must have forgotten to tell you. Seth can make people do whatever he wants them to," She looked back at Seth and gave a disapproving head shake.

"Sorry Carmen, nice to meet you." Seth apologized, looking back at me, and laughed at my confused expression. "I'll leave you two be now." He walked back outside and ran off into the forest towards the lake.

"Don't mind him, he's just annoying," Felix whispered into my ear and turned us around.

"See you soon, Carmen." Both Francis and Alice called out. I could hear the smiles in their words.

Felix brought us out to the garage, gently placed me into the passenger seat of his deep maroon Volvo, and sped around to the driver's side. I turned on the music and laughed when I realized he had put the song he composed for me on a CD and had it in his car.

"I have to have it everywhere, to remind me of you and your beautiful face." He leaned over the middle column to kiss me as he put a hand up to my face and stroked my cheek as he pulled his lips away and set his forehead on mine. "I love you, forever, in all of my immortal life." He smiled.

"And I love you, for all of my boring, mortal life." I slightly lost my smile, and so did he as we realized what I had said.

"Carmen, your mortal life *isn't* boring. You're not supposed to be immortal like me, you're supposed to *age*. You're supposed to *grow*. You're not supposed to know everything inside a book just by touching the cover. *You're normal.*" That was the first time anyone had called me *normal*. Ever since I was young I've been the weird, annoying outcast. Up until I met Felix. If I hadn't met Jenny, Alex, Harley, Michael, or Felix. I'd have no friends, and I wouldn't be happy.

"My mortal life *is* boring. Because that means I can't be with you *forever*. And that's what I want. I want *you*. Forever." My heart was racing, was he going to break up with me because of this? He knew I wanted an immortal life, and I knew he was too scared to allow that to happen to me. I was scared too, but I knew I'd have to become like him for any chance for us to stay together past college, maybe even past high school.

"And I want you forever. It's just that your definition of forever and my definition of forever are two different things, love."

"Then what *is* your definition of forever with me then, Felix?" He pondered and tried to think of an answer. But instead of answering, he turned in his seat and looked straight on.

"We should get going." He said as he turned the engine on.

"Wait," I demanded, trying not to raise my voice. He looked over at me as I continued. "What *is* your definition of forever with me, Felix?" I repeated, demanding to know an answer. If he didn't answer I was thinking of getting out of the car and asking Francis to drive me home. And I knew that Francis or Alice were going to tell Felix telepathically, and that was fine, I needed him to know I **needed** an answer. He cleared his throat and turned back to me slowly.

"My definition of forever with you, Carmen. Is watching you grow old, watching you live your best life. Not an immortal life like myself and my family. I just can't bring myself to imagine you, *my* Carmen, to be a monster like me. Someone who takes away your full purpose of living. Someone who selfishly stays together with you, just because he can't bring himself to hurt you by leaving." He explained his answer in his low, soft voice, closing his eyes after he finished, awaiting my answer.

"My definition of forever with you, Felix. Is us both staying at the beautiful age of 18, for as long as the world exists. I can't imagine you, still a perfect, handsome, hot boyfriend, while I look like a grandma and die slowly. Someone who would be seen as weird to be with someone my age... old, and fragile. Someone who looks as if he could still be in high school or college. Someone, who selfishly wants to be like you, just to not have to risk being hurt by you, or being hurt by time." I explained my definition back to him in the same way he had explained his definition to me.

"Is that really what you want? To get rid of every human experience possible? Like getting married, having a child, seeing your child grow up, etcetera? Just to be with me?"

"Who says we can't get married? Adopt a child? Watch that child grow up. And etcetera. Becoming immortal isn't stopping me from having human-like experiences, I just won't be human."

"Then it's not a human-" He began as I cut him off by kissing him. He was surprised, but kissed back, molding our lips together perfectly.

"I *want* you. **Forever**." I breathed out, releasing our lips and setting my forehead on his.

"I want *you*. **Forever**." He repeated and kissed me again. Not letting me breathe much. After a couple of minutes, he finally let go of the kiss and leaned away slightly. "Let's talk about this later, love." I nodded, leaning away and facing the closed garage door in front of the car.

"We should... Probably go..." I breathed unsteadily from just recovering my breath.

"Yeah, we should." He looked in front of him, and the garage door opened as he pulled out onto the long driveway. He reached his hand over the middle column and held mine. My heart was racing as if I was a 13-year-old holding hands with my middle school boyfriend for the first time.

We arrived at my house, and Felix leaned over the middle column and so did I. Our lips met, and as soon as it started, it was over.

"I gotta get going," I said, pulling away, and rubbing his hand.

"Yeah, me too. Can't wait to see how Francis and Alice react to us sitting in the garage for ten minutes before going." He laughed.

"Yeah, maybe don't tell me how they react, I don't want to know."

"I'm just joking, they don't have a problem with us being together, don't worry." He rubbed my hand and gave it a reassuring squeeze and leaned in to place a kiss on my cheek, but I turned my head, forcing him to kiss my lips. He didn't mind.

"Are my parents gonna be mad about me being gone for so long? I need you to tell me."

"No, love. They won't be even slightly upset after you tell them that you were visiting me and that I was okay. Go along now, they are waiting."

He smiled, and that helped my anxiety. "You'll do great. Keep your window open, and I'll come to see you after it's over. I love you." He called out that last part as I got out and closed the car door, and he drove off after I reached the front door. Dad was sitting on the couch, packing a small bag of things as I walked in. The door closed quietly, but he heard it and turned his head away from the T.V. to face me.

"Carmen! I wasn't expecting you home tonight… And neither was your mother." He walked up to me and gave me a big hug.

"Hey, Dad. Sorry for catching you off-guard. Where is she?" I hugged back, smiling to see Dad so happy.

"Oh, uh. Your mother had to go work a night shift at the hospital, they needed extra help. And as for me, because I bet you're wondering. I have to go and fill in for my friend Tom… You know him… But we both won't be back till probably after 12, maybe later. Sorry, kiddo."

"It's okay, I'm almost 18, have pretty good knife skills, and know how to call 911. Nothing bad is going to happen. I promise." I looked up at the clock. Eight-thirty already? I'm just glad it wasn't dark out. Dad laughed at my expression after I looked at the clock.

"I gotta get going, kiddo. Make sure to get some rest." He let me get past him, and he exited out the door with a smile and a nod. I was kinda upset that Felix hadn't told me that they weren't home.

After I grabbed a snack, I slugged upstairs to my room, and collapsed onto my bed, falling asleep almost instantly. As I realized what dream I was going into, it was too late to wake back up.

Four

"Felix, wait up!" I laughed as we ran through the forest on the cliffs, overlooking the lake below. Felix sped up but came back to me as I stopped and noticed a man in all black appear from behind the trees. I couldn't make out his face. He walked up to us as Felix wrapped an arm around my waist, taking a couple of steps backward.

"Carmen, don't say a word." He whispered in my ear.

"Well, Well, Well. If it isn't Felix and his loving *mate*. I'm so glad to finally meet you two. Felix thinks about you all the time, don't you Felix?" Felix didn't answer and just held me tighter. "How are you guys? Good?" He chuckled an evil laugh, "I hope so... I wouldn't want anyone to feel..." He took a couple of steps forward. "DOWN." He finished, grabbing Felix's neck, and pushing him down to the cold, hard ground as I screamed.

My body wasn't screaming in the dream, It just stood there calmly, and my body in real life was screaming. Loudly. No one was home, so no one would be able to hear my screams and comfort me. I was alone.

"No No, Felix!" I screamed, over and over again. "Felix!" I screamed at the top of my lungs as I watched the scene that had happened 2 weeks ago, unwrapping in my head all over again.

The man in black pushed Felix against a tree, and I swear I heard something crack. He let go of Felix, and Felix fell to the ground with a pained expression as he held his possibly broken head. The man walked up to *me*, put a hand around the side of my neck, and leaned in and sniffed my hair. I saw a flash of something or someone, and I got pushed to the ground, a large wound on my right leg due to a piece of bark or a small stick being slightly shoved into my right thigh. I heard Felix gasp and then saw a small glimpse of him fighting with the man.

Felix was on top of him, beating him with his fists, but soon got overturned by the man and was standing, with the man's hand gripping tightly around his neck.

"Too bad you didn't have the strength to change her. She could be saving you right now. But no, you had to keep her a *fragile,* little-" His words got cut off by Felix's punch to the face. I sat up against the tree and took off my sage green zip-up hoodie, and tied it tightly around my upper thigh as Mom had taught me. I took the piece of wood out of my leg and watched the fight break out. My body in the dream was all calm, and not scared at all, while my body in real life screamed in emotional agony.

Felix and the man were right on the edge as I tried to stand, and my tumbling made Felix lose focus, making the man trip his leg, and causing them to fall twenty-five or so feet into the lake below.

"*Mon soleil,*" He began with something in french, "I love you, *soleil,*" Felix said right before he fell into the lake, his words ringing in my ears as a sad french tune that I didn't know the meaning of.

"No No! Felix! Not again! Not again!" My body screamed as the one in the dream overlooked the lake calmly as if nothing had happened.

I yelled Felix's name loudly, as a sudden warm hand lay on top of mine, rubbing it slowly, and calmly.

"No, no no no. Go away!" I screamed, about to say more but my words got cut off by a calm, soft shushing.

"Shhh," A low voice cooed. "It's okay, I'm here. You just had a nightmare is all, love." At that voice I instantly opened my tear-filled eyes, looking up at the blurry version of Felix, kneeling at the side of my bed, holding my hand.

"F-" I tried to talk, but my voice was on fire, and Felix shushed me. He very quickly flashed to lay behind me, his right arm draping over my body, wiping the tears away with his thumb.

"It's okay, Carmen. I'm here, you're okay, you're alive. There is nothing to worry about, love. You're safe." I sobbed, grabbing onto his hand that was on my cheek, giving it a lot of tiny kisses.

Felix turned the lamp on, and sat up, looking at me shift to sit on top of his lap, taking his face in my hands. "It happened all over again," I explained as I leaned in to kiss him, as he kissed back his hands roamed to my waist, and mine roamed to his soft, dirty blond hair, tugging at it slightly. We kissed for a while. As he finally disconnected he spoke.

"I'm sorry for not getting here sooner, love. Your thoughts are still shielded so I couldn't help, but looking at your future in the next 2 minutes, I came as fast as I could."

"It's okay," I whispered as I kissed him again. This time he didn't disconnect for a while, and he slowly moved his hands up my back, and up my shirt, and I moved my hands down to his chest.

"No, Carmen." He pulled away and pulled his arms out of my shirt slowly. He placed them on my waist again. "We can't go any further." He warned as I groaned softly.

"How about you try to sleep? I'm here, and if you have another nightmare, I won't make you go back to sleep, and we can stay up and watch movies. Okay?" I nodded, got off his lap, and set my head in the nook in between his arm to rest.

"Carmen… Carmen…" A low voice from behind me hummed, and after I didn't answer, he started humming my song.

"Felix," I opened my eyes, turning my body over, and pushing my head into his chest. "5 more minutes." I groaned as he chuckled his low chuckle.

"It's already 8 am, love." He smiled, kissing the top of my head.

"It's too early~" I muttered, putting my left leg on top of his, trying to restrict him from getting up.

"Your parents are going to wake up soon~" He cooed

"Too bad, you can't leave me." I rolled over and climbed on top of him. I connected our lips and his hands moved to my waist.

"I'm not going to leave you. I can stay in your room while you talk to them." He breathed through the kiss. I disconnected our lips and sat back up.

"You better not leave," I threatened, trying to sound serious, but failing by smiling.

"God I love you." He smiled, leaning forward to kiss me again.

"You sure do," I blushed and smiled, kissing him back. His hands disconnected from my waist as our lips did. "I gotta get dressed," I said, both of us looking down at my outfit. I was wearing Felix's *Queen* t-shirt, which was two sizes too big for me, and a pair of black shorts underneath. I swung my body over Felix's lap, and got up to my closet, opening it to find my entire closet filled with Felix's clothes, somehow still clean though.

"So *that's* where all my shirts went!" He laughed and stood up behind me, wrapping his arms around my waist, and looking at the closet.

"I thought you were dead..." I muttered and he laughed.

"Well, when we move we can share a large closet, and you can wear my shirts when-" His words got cut off by his thoughts. He looked blankly at the closet and muttered something under his breath.

"Felix?..." I turned my head to look up at him. His arms tightened around my waist.

"Ah, sorry... um, your mother woke up, you better hurry."

"There's more than that. What happened?" I wanted—No no no, I *needed* to know what had happened—he wouldn't react like that to just finding out Mom woke up.

"I, Uh..." He cleared his throat and stared at the closet again, his arms still wrapped around me tightly. He walked backward and sat us down on the bed gently. He muttered something under his breath and continued staring. I repositioned myself to straddle him, and I set my head on his chest, imagining his nonexistent heartbeat.

"Love, what is it?" He looked at me, set his head on my shoulder, and didn't talk. "Can I know about it? Or is it something to do with you and your family?" He just nodded. "What does that mean? I can't know about it?"

He looked up at me, "I will tell you as soon as I get a clear answer of what's going on from Francis. It's not good, love." He put his head back on my shoulder, and his phone rang. "It's for you. Francis doesn't have your phone number." He muttered into my shirt. I picked up the phone and answered it.

"Francis? Is everything okay? Felix isn't doing too good."

"That's what I called to talk to you about. He has a better vision of people's thoughts than we do because he isn't as old as we are. He saw something really bad in the main *Immortal Leader*'s mind, and we need him here as soon as possible. I know you don't want him to leave before or during telling your parents the plan, so we are willing to wait. You will need to hurry, though."

"Okay, will I be able to hear about this too? Or will I have to stay home?"

"You could come along, it's just you might get bored with all the 'Immortal Talk'."

"That's okay. See you later," I smiled at the fact that I was able to go with him. He said goodbye and hung up, and I put Felix's phone on the bed. I put my arms around his neck, my head in the crook of his neck, and then he laid his head on my shoulders.

"I love you," I whispered into his ear.

"I love you, too." He muttered back to me. We sat like that for a while, and I didn't make an attempt to move, he was thinking, and I was happy that I'd finally get to be around him and his family more since I knew about their secret. Eventually, Felix spoke in his low voice.

"You gotta get dressed, your parents are up and drinking their coffee. Now would be the best time to do this, because they have already decided they will let you move." He muttered, his head still on my shoulders.

"Okay. If you want you can go home and sort things out before I come over." He lifted and shook his head.

"No. I'm going to wait for you. After you tell your parents, and they say you can move, you're going to ask to bring some of your stuff over to my house, and we will leave together."

I got up and walked over to my closet. I picked out two shirts, one was a long sleeve, sage green shirt with a white star in the center, and the other was a white long-sleeve and a black short-sleeve to go on top.

"That one," Felix said, pointing to the green star shirt that was in my left hand. I nodded and hung the other set back up. "The other shirt was something that Ms. Rossum would wear." Ms. Rossum is the very 2000s-style English teacher at school and wears stuff like that, and stuff that old ladies in their 80s would wear even though she's only in her 40s. I laughed and grabbed two pairs of jeans. One bell-bottom pair, and one high rise with holes in the knees.

"High rise…" Felix said before I even turned around to show him the options. "…Ooh! You could pair it with fishnets underneath."

"Are you getting fashion lessons from Carly?" I teased.

"No…" He lied. "Okay fine, Carly and I were talking and she was telling me what to pick. I did pick out the shirt without her help though." He chuckled.

"Fine, I'll wear the fishnets." I rolled my eyes and he smiled. I walked over towards him.

"You don't have-" I cut his words off with a kiss.

"Carly says I do, so I have to. She's so much better at fashion than me." I said, pulling away from the kiss. He smiled.

I turned to my undergarments drawer, pulled out what I needed, and got changed. When I had everything on I sat down at my desk, and did some light makeup, which consisted of some eyeliner made with eyeshadow, mascara, some concealer for under my eyes and over my pimples, and the most important part. Blush. Felix always did this step. He turns my head to look up at him and then kisses me, it makes me blush every time. He always laughs at how fast my face becomes red.

"I love you," He told me as he turned on the record player I had sitting on the desk. The record I had in was the song he made for me. He pulled me up by my waist and started dancing with me. "I had to. You have to do something that I know will cause you anxiety, so I wanted to cheer you up first." He smiled and whispered into my ear. I smiled back and we danced for a little bit. When the song was over he wrapped his arms around my waist tightly and bent down a little bit to kiss me.

"You gotta go talk to them," He started, and I shut him up with a couple of small kisses.

"You better be here when I get back." I smiled.

"Yes ma'am," He laughed as I unwrapped his arms from my waist and pushed him down on the bed.

I blew him a kiss as I walked out the door and closed it behind me. My parents were watching the news when I stepped out of my room.

"Hey, kiddo! Have you seen this?!" Dad asked as I walked down the stairs. "It says Felix is okay! He was reported at The Bartlett Regional Hospital. He's gonna be okay!" Dad stood up and hugged me tightly.

"Yeah, that's what I was going to talk to you about last night." I chucked anxiously after the hug.

"Oh. Well, I would like to hear your side of how you knew and all that." He smiled, sitting back down by Mom. I sat in the yellow chair in the living room and spoke.

"So, I was at Francis and Alice's house, because… They told me Felix was alive, and they wanted to pay… or at least *help* pay for my house, my car, and college. As long as you're both okay with it, at least. And they wanted just to talk, and make sure I knew he was okay. So we went to the hospital he was reported at, and he has to heal…" I paused, trying to think of how to bring this conversation to my house and moving plans with Felix.

"So Francis, Alice, and I were thinking… That while Felix heals, I could send my small stuff to their house, to store there. And when Felix is better in the next week or so we can take that long trip to Fairbanks after school ends in 3 weeks, since It'd be dumb to have to take multiple trips." I picked at my fingernails, and my parents stalled for a second, but then finally replied.

"We say yes. Because your birthday is June 2nd, school ends June 4th, and he should be better in a week… It all lines up and you're lucky." Mom laughed. "But yes, you may slowly bring your stuff over to Francis and Alice's house, and then the day after graduation, if you want to, you can leave. But since you know Felix is okay, we're letting you do all of this. You have to go to school, at least Monday through Thursday. If you want to get out of school this Friday to go visit him, that's fine by me." She smiled, rubbing Dad's arm as if *he* were nervous.

"Really?!" I beamed and stood up as she did, hugging her tightly and laughing. "I need to go tell Francis!"

"Can't you just call him?" Dad asked, probably not wanting me to go anywhere.

"Don't have his phone number. But I'll ask when I'm over. Plus I wanted to see if Carly wanted to go shopping with me, Maybe she can push some fashion sense into me." I laughed, going up the stairs. "Thanks, Mom! Thanks, Dad!" I ran to my room as I heard Dad mutter something.

"She seems way too excited for this…" And Mom replied with something along the lines of; "Shut up, you'd be excited if your mother let you move in with your boyfriend at the age of 17… 18, I should say. God how did she get so-" I closed the door, not wanting to hear anymore. I looked at my Felix, laying on the bed, looking at me with a big smile on his face.

"I told you you could do it!" He got up and picked me up, his arms around my waist, mine on his face. I leaned in and kissed him.

"I'm happy you didn't leave," I admitted, leaning away from the kiss. He placed me down and smiled, flashing over to the bag he packed of mine.

"I threw some money in there since you said you wanted to go *clothes shopping*." I groaned and he smiled. "Carly was already filled in on the important stuff that Francis, Alice, and I will be talking about. Why don't you go have a girl's day with Carly? She'd be so happy!" He smiled and pushed the bag out for me to grab.

"Fine. *Just* so my parents aren't suspicious when I come home with no clothes, *and* to make Carly happy. But you better give me a summary of what happens afterward." I tried to be serious, but couldn't be, with his handsome face smiling at me. *For me.*

"Good, because Carly read my mind, and if you'd said no, she would have made you sometime this week anyways." He turned off the bedside table lamp, and my record player, and went to the window. "I'll be in the car. Tell your parents you're leaving, and that if any plans change you'll text them."

"Okay," I said softly. "I love you," It sounded weird to say when I'd see him in literally 2 minutes, but still, I needed him to know. Forever and always.

"And I love *you*." He grinned, "***Forever.***" He added, climbing out the window and falling to the ground gracefully. He blew me a kiss and flashed to my car. I went out of my room into the hallway, went down the stairs, told my parents what Felix had told me to tell them, and left.

Felix was already in the driver's seat, establishing the fact that *he* was going to drive. He was better at it anyways, so I didn't mind.

"Hey, love." He smiled and grabbed my hand after I'd buckled. I blushed and squeezed his hand.

"So Carly knows we're going shopping?" I asked.

"Yeah, she's getting ready as we speak. Don't worry, you look beautiful, and shopping isn't *that* hard."

"Do *you* want to go shopping with your fashion-obsessed sister? Because I'll gladly let you go." I joked. He smiled bigger than before, started the car engine, and drove away from my house. He tightened his grip on my hand, and stared off, barely paying attention to the road.

"Felix… What is it?" I asked in a soft, caring voice.

"The… The Immortal Leaders… They are coming for *you*." He spoke emotionlessly. Scared, even. I was worried, I'd never seen Felix this scared before. I called Alice and asked for Francis.

"Carmen, what's wrong? Is Felix hurt?"

"*Don't* tell him, Carmen," Felix whispered in his low, warning tone. "Please, love." He looked over at me and squeezed my hand even more.

"Um… I just wanted to ask if I could get your phone number, just so I don't have to call Alice to call you."

"Yes, of course, but are you sure Felix is alright? I can't see his thoughts… or yours for that matter…"

"Yeah, we're okay. We're just driving over to your place right now."

"Okay. I'll see you in a bit then. I'll text you from my phone. Goodbye, Carmen." He hung up and texted me just seconds later. I saved his number as a contact, and shut off my phone, looking over at Felix's emotionless expression.

"Felix, what are you seeing?" I asked calmly and patiently, knowing he was worried.

Five

"It's Floyd... He is coming here... With Esther... To see *you*." his eyes widened, and he started to worry about what they would do to me. "They'll be here June 6th at midnight, on the opposite side of the river." As Felix talked, I wrote this down in my phone's notes. He tightened his grip on my hand, scaring me even more.

I turned on the radio and pressed 'CD', and the radio started playing my song. I hummed along to try and help him calm down, and it slightly worked. His grip released slightly, but he didn't take his eyes off the road.

I hummed the entirety of my song as we drove to their house. Felix parked in the driveway and flashed around to my side to open the door before I could even process what had happened.

"Carly is waiting for you... Don't say a *word* about what happened in the car. I shielded your thoughts for the next two hours so if you think about it that's fine, just *don't* say a word... Please, love." He turned me to face him. He wrapped his arms around my waist as he leaned down and I stepped on my tippy-toes to kiss him. Carly cleared her throat after a while and said;

"Hurry it up, lovebirds!" I blushed and Felix pulled away, placed a small kiss on my forehead, and let go of my waist.

"I love you, *forever*." He smiled, awaiting my blushing.

"I love *you*, **forever**." I let go of his hands and walked over to Carly, who was standing by a blue McLaren, with her arms folded together.

"We're going to have so much fun!" She squealed, pulling me into a hug. Felix laughed from behind us.

"I think *you're* going to have a lot of fun." She laughed and flashed over to the driver's side of the car as I got in.

She turned on the radio and pulled out of the drive. There was some overrated pop song on, but she must have liked it because she kept it on.

"Hey, Carmen. What exactly happened with Felix before you guys got here? He sounded…. Strange on the phone." Felix's warning replayed in my head, and I just answered with a;

"He's okay… He was just worried about something." I smiled, trying to put off a happy tone.

"Why are your thoughts shielded? Felix shielded them. Why?" She looked over at me and turned the radio down, waiting for my answer.

"I'm not exactly sure… He said something about you not being able to stop snooping through my brain."

"I can *so* control myself." She gasped playfully.

"Then why did you notice that?" I asked playfully and she rolled her eyes.

We were silent for the rest of the car trip. Carly pulled into a downtown area outside of Haines. There were clothes stores, coffee shops, grocery stores, bookstores, craft stores, thrift stores, literally everything you could think of.

"Can we *please* go to other stores, not *just* clothing stores? Like a bookstore, or a coffee shop." I begged. She thought for a second and then replied.

"*Fine.* But *only* because I'm such a good friend. But you *have* to try on at least 3 dresses and shoes." She smiled.

"*'Fine.* But *only* because I'm such a good friend.'" I mocked and laughed.

She pulled into a parking spot in front of a small coffee shop. We got out and she just told me to order whatever, and that she didn't want anything. I knew that Immortals didn't eat or drink because ever since I knew about Felix, he hasn't had to pretend. So I just went up to the barista and ordered.

"Hey, could I please get a large, vanilla, iced coffee? The name for the order is Carmen." She pressed buttons on the keypad and the barista behind her grabbed out one of the cups labeled 'large', and started preparing my drink.

"Will that be all?" She smiled a real smile. I nodded and handed her my card. I smiled back. She told us the wait time would only be a few minutes, so Carly and I went to go sit.

Carly listened to the music… and or the baristas' thoughts. I went on my phone and texted Felix. He called me because he enjoyed hearing my voice more than texting.

"Hey, love," he began. "Everything alright?"

"Yeah, I just missed you," I whispered. "Is everything okay over there?" I pursed my lips and my tongue clicked softly.

"Sort of. I'll tell you when you get here." I could hear his smile through his words.

"Okay. I love you… *forever*."

"I love *you*… *forever*." He replied, said goodbye, and hung up. Carly looked at me with a disapproving face as my name was called. I got up, grabbed my coffee, and sat back down by Carly.

"You guys can't even last being without each other for 20 minutes. At least my girlfriend and I are better at hiding the fact we need each other every second of the day." I rolled my eyes and laughed.

"I'll turn my notifications off if that makes you feel better." I took my phone out of my pocket and turned off the notifications. I hoped I wouldn't regret it later, but Carly and I were having a *girl's* day. **Not** a '*sit around and call your boyfriend*-day'. I pocketed my phone and took a sip of my coffee.

"Where are we going shopping?"

"I know you want to go to the bookstore and the thrift store, so we can go there after we go to the dress shop down the street." She smiled, her teeth a perfect paper white.

"Okay," I smiled back, actually excited that we weren't going to spend the entire day dress-shopping. "Thanks," I added. We sat and talked for a little bit, mainly about makeup and fashion. As soon as I finished my coffee, Carly took my hand and raced me out of the store and onto the streets. We decided to just walk to the stores and keep our car parked since it didn't make sense to drive 30 seconds down the street.

"How may I help you two beautiful-" A man with purple and pink eyeshadow, and makeup started to talk, but stopped, looking at Carly and me. He examined us for a second, and then his face beamed with excitement. "Oh! Carly! How are you? You haven't been here in a while!"

"Yeah! Um, I'm alright. This is Felix's girlfriend, we're just having a girl's day." She smiled, wrapping an arm around my shoulders. I smiled, trying to show that I was happy, but according to Felix, I was pretty bad at that.

"If there is *anything* I can help you with, *please* let me know." He moved over a little bit to let us through, and I looked around the store, becoming overwhelmed by the number of clothes, shoes, makeup, and hair products all over the store.

"I- Wow…" I audibly gasped.

"I know right?! This store is the best!" She removed her hand from my shoulder and spun around in the center of the store. "First, we have to look for dresses for graduation!" She grabbed my hand and pulled me to the large collection of dresses in zip-up transparent bags. "What's your favorite color?"

"Dandelion Yellow… Or Sage Green."

"Alright… What's *Felix's* favorite color on you?" She laughed, and that made me know that Dandelion Yellow and Sage Green dresses were a no-go in Carly's world.

"Uhm… I think he's said before that it's like a deep or royal blue." I flushed as she looked through the blue section. She grabbed one off the rack and held it up to me.

"I say you try on this one." She handed the blue dress to me, and smiled brightly, motioning her head to the dressing rooms.

I went into the first dressing room as I heard Carly say 'Oh! This one too!'. I zipped the dress out of its bag, and let the soft cotton prick my fingers. At least she knew that I liked comfy and casual. I pulled off my shirt and my jeans and slid the dress on over myself. It was a medium-length dress. Not too short, and not too long that it dragged on the ground, it ended at about my knees. It had a cute yet casual black ribbon tied on it right underneath my chest. It had no straps and a slight, heart-shaped opening in the back. Carly knocked, and I let her in to look.

"You look *amazing*!" She grinned. "I love the way it curves on you. And oh the back!" She said as I spun around, showing her the exposed back.

"Is this the one?" I laughed.

"I mean, if you don't want to try on other dresses, I'm one-thousand and ten percent okay with this one."

"Then let's get this one." I wanted to go to the bookstore as soon as possible. So the fewer dresses to try on, the better.

"Okay, you can look at shoes while I go look for my dress!" She beamed. I was glad that shopping with her made her happy, and I'm sure Felix was happy that I was keeping her occupied. "Go put that dress on hold with Marcus." I nodded.

Carly left the dressing room, and I took the dress off, pulled my pants on, and pulled my shirt over myself. I put the dress back in its bag carefully and stepped out of the dressing room. I walked over to the counter, and Marcus was standing right there, on the phone with someone. I overheard some of their conversations but didn't pay any attention as I waited.

"Sorry, my husband called. Family problems." He chuckled, "What can I do for you?" He smiled as I handed him the bag with the dress. "Ooh! Good eye!"

"I'm bad at fashion… I just decided to buy the first one Carly picked out." I laughed and whispered jokingly. He put the dress on a hook that had a wooden sign above it that read *'on hold'*. I walked over to Carly, who had a royal-looking purple dress, and a classical golden yellow in the other.

"What one do you think Oliver is going to like? I don't want to disappoint him."

"You will look stunning no matter what, Carly. He loves you, and clothes aren't going to change that." Oliver is Carly's boyfriend, Carly talked about him all the time. I'm not exactly sure how he knows about the Whites, but I just assumed he was immortal, too since they are dating.

"You're right. Thanks, Carmen." She put the yellow one back and hugged me. "I'm glad we could go shopping. Otherwise, you'd probably show up wearing last year's dress!" She gasped and put a hand to her forehead dramatically. I laughed along with her. "Shoe time!" She rushed me over to the shoe section after she had placed her dress down at the counter.

"I think nice, black shoes would suit your dress. You look for some *cute*, comfy shoes for you to wear."

I looked over at the wide collection of shoes and went to the black section. There were platforms, stilettos, and boots. I honestly thought that a low, boot-type shoe would look best, but Carly shook her head when I went in the direction of boots and pointed to the stilettos and high heels.

I looked through them and saw a cute pair of Mary Jane Stilettos and picked them up. They were basic, black high heels, with a wider heel, and a thick black buckle strap a little above where my ankle would end if I were wearing it.

"Ooh, I like those!" Carly was holding 3 pairs of silver heels in her hands. "Help me pick, and then we have to practice walking in them." I picked a pair of shoes similar to mine, just a thinner heel, a thinner strap, and a little diamond accenting in the form of flowers on the side of the shoe on the strap. We went to check out, and I pulled my phone out. 'Three missed calls: Felix♡' and '12 new texts: Felix♡'

"Oh shit," I called Felix back and Carly looked over at me and groaned, but stopped when she saw the look on my face. She ushered me away to take the call.

"Felix? Is everything alright?" My voice trembled.

"Something happened to Felix, you and Carly need to get here as soon as possible." Even when Francis was startled, he still managed to keep calm.

"Okay, she is paying for our dresses now, after we get outside I'll tell her."

"She already knows." He reminded me about the fact they could send messages to each other as long as their mind wasn't shielded.

"Oh right. We'll see you in a little, then. Thank you, Francis."

"Goodbye, Carmen." He hung up and tears started streaming down my cheeks. *This* is why I wanted to stay there and hear what happened. *This* is why Felix and I can't stay away from each other for more than 20 minutes when he's scared and worried. Carly walked up to me and wrapped a hand around my shoulder as we walked out to the car.

"He'll be okay, Carmen. It's okay." She tried to cheer me up, but I couldn't stop thinking about the fact that Felix wasn't okay.

We arrived at the White's house in less than ten minutes, and I raced inside, *needing* to see Felix. *Needing* to see if he was *okay*. I sped into the living room and was met with Felix, sitting on the couch, staring into the distance.

"Felix? Love… Are you alright?" I asked, and he didn't answer.

"He's been like that since you left. What *happened* in the car, Carmen?" Francis asked as he walked into the room. I didn't want to go against what Felix had told me, but I was worried that if I didn't tell Francis the truth, Felix would be in even *bigger* trouble.

"When we got in the car… Felix had seen something. He said Floyd and Esther were coming… for *me*. I don't know why… he wouldn't tell, or maybe he just didn't know. He said they are coming June 6th, and are going to be across the river at midnight. They *won't* be alone." I said that with so much confidence, I had to make sure Seth wasn't in the room.

"That helps a lot, thank you."

"I also think that he may be acting like this because he finally found out what they are going to do, or why they are coming for me." My voice cracked and trembled after the last 7 words.

"I'm going to do some research and talk with Alice a little bit, could you try to snap him out of this? It's alright if you can't." He smiled and left the room.

"Felix, love? I want to try something to help you get back to me." I kissed his forehead and went over to the grand piano across the coffee table, and started playing my song. I hummed along with the piano as tears streamed down my cheeks slowly.

I played the song a couple of times, and eventually heard long, deep breaths, and shuffling, but I kept playing with my eyes closed. Eventually, I heard a low, soft voice start humming along, and I opened my eyes to be met with Felix. His arms snaked around my waist as he pulled me up from the piano seat.

"Hello, my love." His voice was low and scratchy like he had just woken up from 2 days of sleep, but I didn't care. He placed a warm kiss on my lips and smiled. I kissed back immediately, and my hands went straight to his hair. "Carmen…" He groaned and I pulled my fingers out of his soft, dark blond hair and stared into his beautiful hazel eyes.

"I love you," he told me after he pulled away from the kiss and set his forehead on mine. *Forever.* He added.

"I love **you**, *forever.*" I kissed his nose and got off my tippy-toes, standing flat on the floor, with him being an entire head taller than me. We smiled as Francis and Alice cleared their throat, smiling as I blushed.

Six

"I'm glad you're okay, Felix." Alice smiled and walked over to us. Felix's grip on my waist loosened, and he walked us over to the couch.

"Felix, what *exactly* did you see? What happened?" We all sat down on the couches as Francis asked.

"In the car, I saw Floyd and Esther make up their minds about coming here to see Carmen, and they didn't mean it nicely. They settled on June 6th, at midnight, across the river. After Carmen left, I finally got a clear vision of their thoughts and found out what they are planning on doing to her. Esther suggested telling us to make her Immortal, but Floyd decided that he was going to skip the talking step and that she was a risk." I clung to Felix's arm and shifted in my seat.

"What're we gonna do to stop them?" The words escaped my mouth as if they weren't my own. I looked over and saw Seth in the doorway smiling.

"Seth, this is a *serious* moment, there is no need for your mind tricks." Alice raised her voice slightly as she spoke.

"It's okay... really. It is what I was going to ask just... Different."

"I mean, we could try to talk to Floyd. Esther already wants to talk to us, maybe we can convince Floyd to listen."

"That won't work," Francis said with a low, calm tone. "I worked with Floyd and his group before Esther came. He doesn't like to hear people out much. Unless there is a good reason."

"He wants to *kill* Carmen! I think that's a good enough reason to hear us out in itself!" Felix raised his voice and sat up straighter. "I *can't* let them hurt her. I've been waiting much too long to have her, and I can't imagine them touching her." He calmed down a little bit and I rubbed his arm, trying to help comfort him.

"Felix... I guess we can try, but I can't tell you that it'll work." Francis calmly explained to him that if we try this, they could end up being exposed or worse… *killed.* Francis and Alice talked with me and my thoughts on the situation. I explained that as long as they are okay with it, I'm willing to try talking to Floyd and his group. After we finished discussing, Felix and I went to his room to talk alone.

"Call Anastasia and tell her you won't be home tonight because Carly offered to have a sleepover." He pressed his lips to my forehead and we sat down on the bed in his room. I pulled my phone out and called Mom, but she didn't answer. I texted her and told her Carly and I were having a sleepover, and Dad called me.

"Hey honey, your Mom is working late tonight and she couldn't bring her phone. I'm fine with you staying over for a sleepover. I love you!" He hung up, not letting me ask how he was or what was wrong.

I set my phone down on the soft bench at the foot of Felix's bed and turned to face him. He had a worried expression on his face, and I wasn't going to have it. I didn't want our lives to be full of worried expressions due to immortals that want to kill me. I wanted our lives to be full of *each other*.

We were together, for as long as forever. Worrying about things like a group of immortals coming here wasn't better than worrying about the fact that if I don't get turned immortal soon, then I will lose Felix, and he will lose me. We sat for a couple of minutes, just looking at each other. His face calmed and he looked at me with his loving hazel eyes, and I looked back with my 'beautiful sky blue eyes' as he called them. I repositioned myself on top of his lap and wrapped my arms around his neck as I molded our lips together.

"Carmen... No more." He breathed out. "I'm not in a good mood and I don't wanna take it out on you." He moved his hands to my waist and held me there. I leaned my forehead against his, and we sat in silence.

"I love you, I'm sorry-" I began after a while, but was cut off by a kiss.

"I love you, and don't be sorry. It's not your fault, love. I shouldn't be upset when I'm around you." I blushed and set my forehead back on his. "I think it's sleep time for the human." He smiled, laying me down on the bed with himself next to me.

"But I'm not tired~" I groaned as he kissed my forehead.

"Too bad, just lay here and I bet you'll be asleep in no time." I groaned again, but he put his arms around me and cuddled me to his chest. I yawned and he rubbed my cheek with his thumb. He started humming my lullaby and I was asleep in no time.

Even with Felix around me, the nightmare came back. I was suddenly falling off a cliff. "No, No, No NO!" My body screamed, and my nightmare backed up, and I had to rewatch the scene all over again.

"Well, Well, Well. If it isn't Felix and his loving **mate**. Felix thinks about you all the time, don't you Felix?" Felix didn't answer, his body in the dream just stood behind me, gripping my waist tighter. "How are you guys? Good?" He chuckled an evil laugh, "I hope so... I wouldn't want anyone to feel..." He took a couple of steps forward toward us both and completed his sentence. "DOWN." He grabbed Felix by the neck and I screamed, I screamed and screamed until my voice was scratchy and hoarse. A sudden warm embrace held me, and a hand stopped me from hitting the bed.

"Carmen, It's okay, I'm here, you're alright." I pulled on his hand, not realizing it was his at first, but I calmed down, settling into his grasp. He squeezed me tighter and hummed my song, trying to help me calm down. "We gotta get these nightmares under control." He murmured into my neck.

"I-I'm sorry," I sobbed, "I don't know why this keeps happening. I know that y-you're okay, but it just keeps happening. My brain likes to remind me of the pain I felt... I guess." I choked out, trying my hardest to not cry so much, but it was hard.

"It's okay, love. Cry all you need, I'd be crying for months if I saw that happen to you." He rubbed my face, wiping the tears away. "We can stay up and watch some movies if you'd like. But we've gotta find a way to stop these nightmares from happening, Carmen." I nodded and sat up, laying my head on his chest. He reached over to his bedside table and grabbed the TV remote for his large, 80" flat-screen.

"What do you want to watch?" He asked, playing with my hair.

"You," I said, climbing onto his lap as he sat up. I kissed him and he immediately kissed back. He breathed out for a second, but immediately hooked our lips together. We kissed for a few minutes and he held onto my waist tightly, as if we hadn't kissed or seen each other in weeks. He tried to lean away, but I pressed my open mouth against his lips, muffling his groans. After a while, we finally pulled away, our foreheads leaned against each other, and we both breathed shakily.

"I love you." I breathed out, smiling.

"I love you, too." He returned the smile and set a soft kiss on my forehead. He sat up, leaning his back against his headboard with me still in his lap. "But seriously, what do you want to watch, love?"

"Doesn't matter to me. I won't be paying much attention anyways." He laughed and kissed me. He turned on some random movie, and I stayed on his lap, with my head on his chest, imagining his nonexistent heartbeat and listening to his slow, deep breathing. He placed a kiss on the top of my head and rubbed circles on my back.

I eventually fell asleep on top of him, and when I awoke he was sitting at his desk writing something., the TV playing soft, calming music.

"Felix?" I sat up and he flashed over beside me.

"Hey, love. Sleep well?" He kissed me and sat me on his lap.

"Yeah… what're you doing?" I flashed my eyes over to his desk.

"I was just writing an email to the school about the fact we will be back tomorrow. I explained the situation and they said we won't have to make up the work as long as we attend every day 'till graduation." He smiled.

"Don't remind me about graduation" I groaned.

"How did our senior year go by so fast? It feels like just a month ago I met you and instantly fell in love." He ignored what I had said and I blushed, but also got lost in thought in what *actually* happened a month ago... The worst day of my life. The day I thought Felix had died. He sensed what I was thinking and kissed me. "Love, it's okay. I'm here and you'll *never* have to go through something like that again. I *promise*" I kissed back and then pulled away, with a blush and a smile on my face.

"You gotta go home soon. Most sleepovers only last 'till 2 pm at the latest." I groaned and my smile decreased.

"Fine." I sighed, getting off his lap and making sure I had everything. He flashed to my side and held me by my waist.

"I didn't mean right now. Unless you want to go home, of course."

"Why would I *ever* want to leave you?" I smiled, wrapping my arms around his neck.

"I don't know, and I hope I never find out." He smiled back, leaning down to kiss me as a knock at the door was heard. He kept his hands around my waist and I kept my hands around his neck as Alice came in.

"Carmen, your mother called. She's wondering if you're okay, and when you're coming home." She smiled at us.

"I'll text her, I was planning on leaving anyway. Thanks, Alice." I smiled back at her and she left, closing the door.

"I guess you gotta go." Felix sighed, letting go of me.

"Yeah, you can drive me. Since my Mom is a part of the PTA group at school you're gonna have to talk to them either today or tomorrow, because I just know you and I returning is going to be news for the next couple of days, then everyone will move on and talk about graduation."

"I'll drive you home and talk to your parents." He grabbed my messenger bag, handed it to me, held my hand, and took my phone out of my back pocket for me.

"Thanks," I smiled and he kissed my forehead.

We got out to the car and Felix opened my door for me and then flashed to the driver's side. As soon as we got in Felix leaned over the middle column and kissed me. He then set his hand in mine, starting the car as I turned on the radio. I set it to a local pop station and it was playing some random songs from the 2000s.

We mainly drove in silence, except when *Party in the USA* came on and we both started singing like little kids. But other than that we didn't talk much. His grip tightened every now and then, I thought maybe he was seeing something, but because he didn't bring it up, I didn't ask.

When we arrived at my house, Felix got out and sped around to the other side, opening my door and helping me get out by taking my hand. He walked up to the front door and knocked, even though it was *my* house. After he knocked I just went in.

"Why'd you knock, Carmen? You live-" Mom began as she looked over. "Felix! I'm so glad you're okay!" She got up and hugged him but backed away after a second, realizing she had just hugged a high schooler.

"Thank you, Mrs. Brooks, and I don't mind a hug. Just so you know." He smiled, taking my hand in his again.

"We were worried sick until we saw it on the news and Carmen came home crying, telling us you were okay."

"Mom... you didn't need to expose me like that..." I muttered as Felix laughed, squeezing my hand tightly.

"Well, I'm just glad you're okay. If you would like to spend some time upstairs until Chris gets home I'm alright with that."

"That works perfectly. We were planning on telling you guys something anyway." He smiled and nodded at Mom when he walked us up the stairs to my room.

"I always forget how pretty your room is, Carmen. It resembles you perfectly."

"The overall colorfulness or the prettiness?" I raised an eyebrow as we went to sit on my bed. My room was extremely colorful, with a yellow bedspread and different rainbow-colored pillows. My bookshelf is a light wood color with a lot of books in rainbow order along with plants. My white desk, with a white monitor and keyboard on it, with a colorful mousepad, books, and plants on top.

"Colorfulness. Your room is nowhere near as pretty as you." He smiled, tilting his head down to my lips, and placing a soft kiss upon them. I blushed, as is obvious, and kissed back, grabbing his hair as he grabbed my waist. There was a knock at the door, Felix finished kissing me and still sat how we were sitting before the knock. Mom walked in and smiled.

"Chris is here if you want to talk to us right now."

"Thank you, Mrs. Brooks. We'll be down in a second."

"Please, call me Ana." Mom closed the door and Felix immediately went back to kissing me. He could tell I was nervous.

"They aren't going to be upset, you're okay, don't worry, love." He breathed out as he set out foreheads together. He grasped my hand and placed a soft kiss on it. "Let's go," He smiled, holding my hand and standing up. I did a couple of breathing exercises that I've known since I was young, and we went downstairs.

"Felix! I'm glad you're okay." Dad said as he shook hands with Felix.

"Thank you," Felix began as he sat us down on the orange couch we had. "I just wanted to come here and explain our plan for after school ends. I'm aware that Carmen has told you the basics, but I just wanted to answer any potential concerns or questions." He smiled, squeezing my hand as we awaited their replies.

"She told us some of it, but we sure do have questions." Mom returned his smile. "Where exactly is this house?"

"It's a cottage in a small forest previously owned by Francis up in Fairbanks. It's about 15 minutes from the University, and I'd be bringing one of my cars, of course."

"Since Fairbanks is really far away, will you two be coming home for the holidays?"

"That is our plan, yes." Felix nodded, speaking with a gentle tone.

"Will you be driving there?" Dad chimed in. This and the fact it's 12 hours away were his only concerns.

"Yes, we will be driving there. I'll keep her safe and if anything goes wrong, you two will be notified." He smiled and squeezed my hand tighter.

"I say yes, then." Dad returned his smile and relaxed in his seat.

"I say yes as well. As long as you guys invite us to family gatherings. I wouldn't mind flying out a little way to see you two." My mother replied.

"Great, then I best get going. Carmen, you should get some rest, You didn't sleep much last night." He looked at me and kissed my forehead after he stood up. "Thank you for your time, Mr. and Mrs. Brooks." Felix nodded toward them and went to the door.

"Thank you for taking the time to talk to them, Felix." I followed him, waiting for him to 'leave' and then climb into my window.

"No worries, I'll pick you up before school and we can go grab some coffee." He smiled, grabbing my hand and waist and leaning down to kiss me. "I love you. *Forever*." He let go of me and walked out the door.

"I love *you*. *Forever*." I called out behind him.

I went upstairs to my bedroom and closed the door. I walked over to my window and saw Felix's Volvo speed away. I reached my hand over to turn on my record player that sat by my window on a nice white cart. My song was playing, it was one of the only two records I owned, so it was on repeat almost all the time.

I went over to sit on my bed and possibly go to sleep. I stayed up for a while, thinking about why Felix actually left when we both wanted him to stay. Thinking about what exactly he was doing, and how this move was going to work out. Eventually, I fell asleep, listening to the sounds of soft rain outside, and my song playing the perfect loop on vinyl like it has when played on CD or played by Felix himself. The nightmare came back, but someone must have read my mind because someone's hand touched my own as soon as the nightmare began.

"Carmen," A stern voice began. It didn't sound like Felix at all. It wasn't even male. "Oh, how glad I am to finally meet you. Must be a shame that Felix *isn't* here to comfort you, hmm?" I sat up, scared as could be. I tried taking deep breaths but my heart was pumping so fast. "Don't worry about what happened, we took care of him." I didn't know what she meant, but I was scared. I screamed at the top of my lungs but she put a hand over my mouth.

"No, No, FELIX!"

Seven

"Carmen, love, what's wrong? Are you okay?" Felix raced over to my side. I had tears in my eyes and I couldn't stop screaming. "This is what I get for leaving you alone, I guess." He muttered, placing his hand on top of mine. "We gotta get this sorted out with Francis. I'm bringing you tomorrow."

"No, No I'm-" I started, still crying and not being able to control my breath.

"Don't say you're fine. You've been having these nightmares for weeks now, love."He wiped the tears from my eyes and placed a kiss on my hand. "I'm going to lay with you, and you're going to try to sleep again, okay?"

"N-no, I-I can't… I don't want to have another nightmare, Felix." I choked out, struggling to form a complete sentence.

"Can you *try*? For *me*? *Please*, love. I'll be right here if anything happens." He repositioned his body behind mine and wrapped his arms around me. He hummed my song along with the tune on the record. I sobbed, trying to hold it in but it all came out.

"Felix… when are they coming?"

"June 6th. We'll stay here until it's over, and then we'll be moving." He placed a kiss on my cheek. "Time to sleep now, love."

"Okay," I breathed out, closing my eyes and turning around, pushing my head into his chest. His breathing was calm and collected, and mine was static and uneven.

After I awoke, Felix still had me clenched to his chest and was still humming.

"Felix?" I murmured into his chest.

"Yes, love?" He placed a kiss on my head.

"What time is it?"

"Ten thirty-two. Why, exactly?"

"We have school!" I muttered some swear words under my breath and tried to sit up, but Felix restricted me.

"It's the last week of school, it doesn't start 'till 11, love. Though I do think we- you… should get ready."

"In a minute," I muttered, snuggling back into his chest. He laughed.

After a good 5 minutes, Felix sat me up. "We gotta get up, Carmen." I groaned, sitting on his lap with my head still on his chest as he kissed the top of my head. He sat me up to look at him. "You wanted to go to school so badly 5 minutes ago. What's wrong?"

"Tired, unmotivated… Worried." He raised an eyebrow at the 'worried' I added. "I'm worried about how people are going to react to us coming back to school. I don't want to be stared at like we just started dating again."

He laughed, remembering the stares we got on the first day our relationship was public to the school, and how I hid in his arms to avoid being looked at.

"It'll be okay. I *promise.*" He smiled his perfect smile, showing his amazingly white teeth mixed with his soft, light pink lips. I got off his lap and went to my closet.

"Help me choose what to wear," I demanded, yet smiled along with him.

"Oh, of course, your majesty." He laughed, walking up behind me and wrapping his arms around my waist. "Hmm… That one." He pointed to a purple tank top. "Paired with those." He pointed to a pair of black sweatpants. "I know you're tired so I'm not gonna make you look appealing to *everyone*." He laughed, "Just appealing to *me*."

I blushed, smiling at him. I got my clothes on and then sat down at my makeup desk. I looked at myself in the mirror, cheeks red, my under-eyes visible, and small pimples scattered on my forehead, nose, and chin.

"Carmen… You're beautiful, okay? No need to worry about your slight flaws, you're gorgeous and I couldn't be luckier to be dating someone as elegant as you, love." He turned my head to kiss me, adding a blush to my face.

"I think I'm gonna skip the makeup step." I talked to myself out loud.

"Good, because you're gorgeous already. You don't need makeup." He stood me up and leaned down to kiss me, interlocking our lips as he wrapped his arms around my waist tightly.

"Okay seriously, you gotta go. You gotta wait outside and then 'pick me up.'" I whispered, breathing shakily. Mom knocked on my door and then Felix was gone in a flash out my window.

"I'm getting ready!" I told her, and she walked in anyways.

"Felix picking you up?" She raised an eyebrow.

"Yeah, we're gonna go grab a coffee first."

"Alright, Stay safe, and have a good day at school. I love you." She exited and Felix came back through the window with a flash.

"I'll go pull my car around, see you in a second."

He flashed out again before I could even say a word. I grabbed my bag and headed out of my room. Dad was on the couch watching the TV as I said goodbye. He said to have a good day, and not get into trouble.

When I got outside Felix's car was already there and he was standing over by my door. Before I even got to the end of the sidewalk, he opened my door and ushered me inside.

He flashed over to the other side and started the car. He reached his hand over the center column and took my hand in his.

"Starbucks or a local coffee shop?" He asked, not remembering which one I prefer.

"Starbucks, please," I said, smiling at him.

We ordered my drink and pulled up to

"Felix White?!" The barista asked, with a surprised look on her face.

"Yeah, that's me." He chuckled, grabbing the drink out of the barista's hand and giving it to me. He squeezed my hand tighter and smiled at me.

"Is that Carmen?" A sour look crossed her face.

"Yes, this is my *girlfriend* Carmen. Have a good day now." He noticed I was annoyed at what expression she had made when asking about me, and that I was uncomfortable. He rubbed my hand with his thumb and kept driving. "How is it?" He asked after I took my first sip, his eyes still on the road.

"It's good, but that's expected. This is like the only drink I get from Starbucks." I reached the drink out to him and he took it from me, took a small sip, and handed it back.

"It's not bad, just not used to drinking or eating much, you know?" He smiled.

We pretty much sat in silence for the rest of the drive. He held my hand and asked a couple of questions, but that was it. When we arrived at school Jenny and Michael were standing by Jenny's car talking and laughing. Felix pulled into the spot next to them and I waited for him to open my door.

"Carmen! I'm so glad you're here!" Jenny ran up to me after I got out and gave me a hug. "How are you?"

"I'm alright, how're you?" I smiled, glancing over at Michael.

"I'm doing amazing now that I know you and Felix are okay." She looked up at Felix and smiled, he returned her smile and reached to grab my hand.

"Hey, Carmen. Hey, Felix." Michael walked up to us and put a hand around Jenny's waist.

"Hello, Michael." Felix cleared his throat. Michael laughed at his formality and I shot an evil glance at him, making him flush and stop laughing. "We have got to go to class now, we'll see you at lunch?" Felix offered, even though he knew I wanted to sit by Carly, her boyfriend, Josh, and Seth. I smiled at Jenny and Felix wrapped an arm around my waist, walking us toward the school.

"I know you don't want to sit by them, but you haven't been to school in a week, love. Plus the only people you've talked to are me and my family. You should sit by your friends."

"But I promised Carly and Oliver I'd sit by them." I groaned, looking up at his perfect face.

"I know, Carmen. But they'll understand."

"*Fine.* But you better come over tonight, for real. Not sneaking through my window."

"Alright, love. You're super easy to negotiate with." He pointed out and laughed. He tilted his head down a little to kiss the top of my head as we walked into Science. Felix talked with Mrs. Gearey about our absence and she said to just sit together at the back table. We were a couple of minutes early, so we just sat and talked as we held hands.

Felix made a quirky remark about school and I laughed louder than I expected, so it caused us both to laugh about that and then for us to laugh about us laughing at my laugh. It was pretty funny, but we were told to simmer down before class started. People walked into the classroom and stared at us.

Felix squeezed my hand and whispered promises in my ear, along with what everyone was thinking about us being back. There were only a couple of negative comments, mainly people wishing that Felix and I had broken up due to all of this and stuff along those lines.

Classes went by pretty fast, and before I knew it, it was lunch. Felix walked me down with an arm around my waist. We passed by Carly and Oliver but Felix must've told Carly I wouldn't be sitting with them because they smiled as we walked past. A couple of kids were staring at us as we walked through the cafetorium, but Felix just held me closer.

"You're being very protective today." I pointed out and he smiled.

"You were worried." He looked over at me.

"That's not all. I think *you're* worried." I smiled back playfully.

"Carmen... I've been around for 304 years... You think I'm worried about people looking at us?" He whispered in my ear, sending shivers down my spine. He laughed when my face flushed a bright pink. We got to the lunch table and Jenny, Michael, Harley, Alex, and Kaleb were there.

"Carmen!" Harley yelled, causing some more people to look over.

"Hey, Harley." Felix let go of my waist as Harley hugged me.

"How are you?"

"I'm alright, how about you?" Felix laughed at my lack of skills for small talk, and I heard Carly and Oliver laughing from behind him.

"I'm doing great. Jenny and I got the big speech we're working on for graduation." She glanced at Felix and smiled. "I'm glad you're okay, Felix."

"Thank you, Harley." he returned her smile and pulled me down by my waist to sit by him. He scooted my chair over with his leg so the chair was right next to him. I leaned into him as he wrapped an arm around me.

"Are you ever going to tell me how you became immortal?" I asked, whispering in his ear.

"Maybe, Carmen. It's just…" He stalled, his low whisper still sending shivers down my spine. "My origin story isn't as fun as you think…"

"Well… I want to know."

"Maybe sometime… Let's just focus on human things right now… Okay, love?" I nodded, relaxing back into him, listening to the graduation things everyone was talking about.

"Oh! I thought I'd invite everyone… we're having a party at my house after graduation!" Carly exclaimed excitedly. She grabbed Oliver's arm and smiled.

"At like… Dr. White's house?" Jenny's eyes were wide. No one had seen their house other than me.

"Yeah! It'll be fun. I already got Francis, er… our Dad's permission." She corrected herself, looking over at Felix as he nodded.

"Do you want anything to eat, love?" He whispered, moving the hair that was in front of my ear.

"Not really," His thumb stroked my cheek and I reached my hand up to hold his but he moved his hand down around my waist again as my cheeks flushed an even brighter pink. Carly went on about the graduation party, but I wasn't listening until she cleared her throat and stopped my daydreaming.

"You're going to be there too, right Carmen?" She repeated, smiling

"Oh, Uh yeah… I'll be there." I cleared my throat and relaxed back into Felix's lap as he rubbed my side.

The lunch bell rang and now I had math, the only class I don't have with Felix since now is his prep hour. Felix walked me there and then set a reassuring kiss on my forehead.

"You'll be okay. I love you. **Forever**." He smiled.

"I love *you*. **Forever**." I stood on my tippy-toes to kiss him as he leaned down, molding our lips together.

"I gotta go. You'll be back to me before you know it." He let go of my waist and hand and then walked away. I walked into class and Mr. Martin told me to just sit at an empty desk. Math was pretty boring, but luckily Jenny came to sit by me, so it wasn't all bad. A couple of people were whispering about me, but I didn't pay attention to them. Mr. Martin gave us this week to play games, so I was just drawing, listening to music, and talking to Mr. Martin, as everyone else, including him, were playing games.

After class was over Felix was standing right outside the door, he grabbed my hand and pulled me aside.

"We need to leave. Now." He gripped my hand tightly, making my expression change from happy to see him, to as worried as could be. "I'm sorry if I'm scaring you, it's just what's happening isn't good. We've got to go get everyone. I'll get Seth and Josh, you get Carly and Oliver." I nodded and he flashed past me. I sped down to Science and told Carly. She tried telling Oliver to stay but I insisted that he come.

"Francis is calling in for all of us. We gotta leave."

"Felix… What's going on?" Oliver asked.

"I can explain it in the car." He gripped my hand and sped to the car, everyone followed behind. "Carly and Oliver, ride with me and Carmen. Josh and Seth can ride together." He ushered me into the passenger seat as Seth and Josh nodded, getting in Josh's car.

"Felix. What's happening?" I answered, gripping his hand over the middle column of his car when he got in. I tried comforting him by rubbing the back of his hand with my thumb, and it kind of worked.

"Esther is sending someone to check in on us."

"Esther? Like Floyd's 'minion' Esther?" Oliver asked.

"Yeah, she's sending some newer immortal. I told Francis and he said we needed to keep Carmen safe and go home." He paused, probably getting information from Francis or someone. "They'll be here at midnight, across the river." His grip tightened on my hand, and I tried to hide the small amount of pain it was causing.

"Felix, release your grip, you're hurting her," Carly spoke up.

"Sorry, love." He let go of my hand but I grabbed it back.

"You need something to grab onto other than your steering wheel, Felix. It doesn't hurt that bad."

"No, Carmen," He tried protesting, but I just grabbed onto his hand, trying to not let him let go. His eyes were focused on what looked like the road but was really inside his mind. He was probably trying to talk to Francis or find more information, or *anything*.

"Francis says that Esther and her minion are willing to chat with us. They aren't going to hurt us unless we hurt them… Or if they don't trust us." Felix gripped his steering wheel tighter.

"Felix… You're going to break that steering wheel." I pointed out, rubbing the back of his hand.

"It's better than breaking your hand, Carmen." I shook my head.

"I don't mind. You don't need to break your perfectly good-" I began.

"I *do* mind. I *can't* hurt *you*, love."

"Felix, she isn't willing to drop this conversation, I'd just follow what she says," Carly smirked. Felix exhaled hard and loosened the grip on his steering wheel and moved his strength over to my hand. I winced a tiny bit but concentrated on the fact that this was better than Felix breaking his steering wheel off.

We arrived at the White's house shortly before that, and Felix flashed over to my side and grabbed my hand, rushing me inside. We walked into the living room and Francis looked worried.

"Francis, explain to them what you had explained to me… *please.*" Felix sat me down but kept standing himself.

"Esther is sending someone by the name of Freya, who is apparently her daughter. Freya is a newer immortal, but from what I can see she is pretty harmless. She isn't the strongest, but she has powers, that's the only reason why Esther has her. She and Esther will be coming at midnight, across the river. We need to get our story together on why Felix and Carmen's faces were all over the town's news. We need to explain that Carmen isn't immortal because there isn't a *reason* for her to be immortal." He looked over at me.

"We need to explain our reasoning, but they don't want me to be talking the whole time, so we need our story to be the same for everyone to explain, without it being too obvious. Felix and Carmen will have to explain why they are together, and that Carmen *won't* be a danger to the other Immortals. If they don't listen, we don't really have another choice other than to fight." Felix sat down by me and grabbed my hand.

"But you said Freya wasn't harmless."

"She'll only fight if instructed by Esther. Floyd doesn't know this is happening, if he did he would probably kill both Esther and Freya right on the spot." Alice walked in and took a seat next to Francis.

"Freya has a power. Every different group does. Our power in this family is mind control. Most of us can read minds, but Seth can control your mood and your thoughts, and Felix can see plans before they happen and read your every thought." Alice began, letting Francis take over the rest.

"Freya's power is unknown, at least to us. No one knows what clan she comes from. We can't read her mind, either. She doesn't come from Floyd's clan, because Floyd doesn't see her powers as useful compared to his."

"Could you check for her power in Esther's mind? She must know if she thinks she's so useful." I asked.

"Esther blocked her mind. She knows we are watching her." Felix answered, "I can't see future plans with her either."

"Carmen, we're going to have to make an excuse on why you can't go home tonight," Francis instructed.

"But my parents aren't going to-" I began, being cut off by Felix.

"Tell them that you're getting stuff ready for your birthday. It's in a day, they can't really tell you no." Felix rubbed my hand and I nodded.

"Could you go call them?" Francis asked in a calm, serious tone. I nodded and stood up, Felix followed so I went to his room.

I pressed call and Mom instantly answered. "Carmen, where are you? The school called saying that Francis ordered you out?"

"Mom, I'm okay. Carly had a birthday planning *emergency.* I'll be back home tomorrow after school."

"Oh, that's fine I guess. Have fun birthday planning. I love you."

"Love you too, bye Mom." I exhaled and ended the call. Felix immediately turned my head to look up at him. He leaned in, placing a kiss on my lips.

Eight

"I'm sorry for scaring you." Felix breathed as he pulled away from our kiss. He wrapped his arms tighter around my waist and pulled me close, setting his forehead on mine.

"We gotta get back out there," I muttered, trying to pull away but he kissed me again, interlocking our lips. Since his door was open I was worried that everyone could see us, but Felix didn't seem to care.

"Alright, we should get back." He grabbed my hand and walked me back to the living room.

"What'd they say?" Francis asked though he knew what she had said.

"I'm allowed to stay to 'get my birthday party ready.'" I used air quotes and Francis laughed.

"Alright, so they'll be here at midnight to talk, if anything involving fighting happens, Felix, you'll bring Carmen home and stay there with her until it's all sorted out. Okay?" Felix nodded as he sat us back down on the couch across from Francis, Alice, and Seth. "Felix, what is it?" Francis asked, looking at Felix's focused face.

"They are on their way." He got out of his mind and looked at Francis.

"But it's not even 3 pm!" Carly pointed out.

"They're all the way in Lower Canada, if they don't make any stops then they should be here by about nine. Nine-thirty at the latest." Francis' eyes glanced over at me.

"What do we do?" I asked. A million things were running through all of our heads. What were they going to do if they didn't believe or trust us? We know that Freya and Esther are willing to listen, but for how long?

"Carmen… There isn't much that *you* can do, I'm afraid." Francis looked over at Felix and he nodded. Felix stood us up and then walked us to his bedroom.

"You and I are going to stay here from now till after they leave... unless there is a fight, then Francis will tell me, and we will leave for your place. To keep you and your parents safe." He grabbed my hands. "If we do have to retreat to your place, we will have to tell your parents. We can either say that Carly didn't need any more help, or that the rest of it was a surprise."

"Okay…" I whispered, scared as could be. He sat us down on his bed after he closed the door.

"They are going to go out and get ready just in case there is a fight. I suggest that *you* sleep." He smiled, trying to cheer me up, but it didn't work much. He pulled me up in between his legs and wrapped his arms around my waist, setting his head on my neck. I placed my arms over his.

"I love you," I reminded him, rubbing his arms with my thumbs.

"I love you, too." He murmured into my neck, placing tiny kisses everywhere. We sat like that for close to 30 minutes, but he repositioned his body to lie down, and he turned over, me still in his arms. He put me in front of him, hummed my song in my ears, and whispered goodnight messages every now and then until I fell asleep.

"Carmen, love…" He cooed, "Time to wake up~"
I groaned.

"What time is it?"

"Almost nine… They should be here soon." He grabbed my waist and pulled me on top of him. I put my head on his chest and he rubbed my back.

"It'll be okay, love."

I realized I was crying as he said that. It was quiet at first but soon got louder and louder, heavier and heavier. He shushed me and started humming again, but it wasn't helping. I was scared… Terrified even, but I mean, who wouldn't be scared after finding out two immortals that could kill you instantly were after you?

"Love, it's alright." He cooed. He tried whispering sweet nothings and humming, but not even he could calm me down.

"Felix…" I tried getting out but it was muffled and scratchy, so I just decided not to talk. There was a knock at the door and Francis peeked his head in.

"You two alright?" He smiled.

"Yeah, she's just worried. Get ready, they just entered Haines."

"Alright. Thank you, Felix. You know what to do." He nodded. Francis excused himself out the door and I instantly started sobbing again. I didn't know why I was crying so much. This wasn't even the big event.

"Shhh. Love, it's alright." He rubbed circles on my back.

"I-I'm sorry… I don't know why I'm crying so much." I tried to calm my breathing by taking deep breaths.

"*Don't.* Don't be sorry. You're *human*, you're allowed to feel scared and pained. I don't mind seeing you upset, it makes you even more comfortable to be around." My crying slowed down and I kept taking deep breaths as he continued rubbing circles in my back. Eventually, I stopped crying and was relaxing on Felix's chest. We sat like that for a while, but Felix's face grew scared, causing me to sit up.

"Freya requests to see you." He looked at me with fright in his eyes. "She says if she doesn't then they will fight to see you."

"Well, then we have to go out, don't we?" He nodded and stood us up. We walked to the back door and he went first, still holding my hand. Freya and Esther were standing across the river, looking at us. We walked up to everyone and I collected my breathing.

"Dear, *Carmen*… We've been waiting to meet you ever since Felix and you went all over this lovely town's news..." Esther began, looking over at Freya. She nodded and Freya walked forward a little bit.

"Carmen... What makes you think it's a good idea to date an *immortal*? We would love to know your thought process." Her eyes skimmed over Felix's family. "We won't hurt her..." She began, reading their thoughts. "Unless we have to." A small smile formed on her lips. I shifted myself to stand behind Felix, my head just barely peeking out behind his back.

"Don't you take another step," Felix instructed Freya to not move, glancing at her harshly.

"Felix... You can't protect her forever. If we don't get this sorted through today then Floyd is going to fight with you guys." She smiled.

"There will be no fighting." Francis cut in.

"If you say so." She took another step, now right on the edge of the river. "We would hate for someone to become *paralyzed* in the fight." When she said the word 'paralyzed' Felix froze. His tight grasp on my arm loosened, and his face relaxed.

"No!" I exclaimed, looking at Freya directly for the first time. Her black, soulless eyes popped out against her pale white skin.

"Carmen, don't stare at her!" Carly warned. I changed my glance over to her. "She has certain powers… That can… severely damage a human…" My gaze flashed over to Freya again. She smiled a wide, toothless smile. Felix collapsed to the floor and I was at his side in a second.

"Please! Please… Don't do this!" Her eyes widened and Felix gasped and his eyes closed. "No! No! Please, stop!" She stopped and looked over at Esther.

"Continue on, love." Esther smiled, her white teeth glowing.

I grabbed Felix and looked at him. His eyes fluttered closed. "No, No, No!" I yelled, looking over at Freya and Esther.

"Freya, let's see if she'll talk now." Esther directed her to stop. Freya looked at her and then back at me.

"Please… Hurt me… Not him." I stood up and took a step closer to the river, looking down at my reflection. "When I first met Felix, I didn't know he was immortal, and it stayed that way for over a year. It only changed because he jumped off a cliff, saving me from… someone." Felix got up and stood next to me, grabbing my hand in his.

"Damen, the guy that we saw that day, is Esther's love. They've been together for as long as I can remember. If we tell Esther that Damen was after you, they should leave you alone." He whispered to me, and then turned back to Freya and Esther.

"Damen was after her. He heard us running through the woods together, about to go cliff jumping… He tried to hurt Carmen, so a fight broke out, and it led to him pushing both of us off a cliff. She didn't know then, but I couldn't bear her staying away from everyone and everything over my 'death', so we told her. I swear she wouldn't have ever known unless necessary, and I consider *that* necessary. I'm sure you two do as well." Freya and Esther exchanged a glance.

"Damen… was *after* you?" Esther asked me as I looked at Felix.

"Yeah I got a bad cut in my leg due to some bark or a branch or something." I grasped Felix's hand tighter.

"I would love to *see* this memory." Freya looked at Felix. "Would you mind me looking?" She turned her gaze to me.

"She's like us I suppose… she controls the mind with one touch or glance," Felix explained and Freya smiled, flashing over across the river

"Although I need consent and a hand to your heart for me to see. Do I have your consent?" I nodded slowly and Felix squeezed my hand, letting go after. She placed her icy cold hand on my chest and I gasped.

"Hmm… Felix means a lot to you, doesn't he?" I nodded. "I see some spots in your mind I can't quite see, that is very odd…" She took her hand off my heart and flashed back over to Esther and Esther nodded.

"Freya can't quite see anything other than what happened… This has never happened before… I suppose we will have to tell Floyd and make him see for himself. I think we best get going… We hope to not have to show up unannounced again." Esther forced a smile

"We hope so too. Thank you, for taking the time to talk things out with us, it really means a lot." Francis returned her smile and they walked away.

"Felix, are you okay? Did she hurt you?" I panicked, taking his face in my own and kissing him a couple of times before he placed his hands on my face, pulling me away.

"I'm okay, Carmen… I'm alright." He wrapped his arms around my waist and held me close, placing a kiss on top of my head.

Felix nodded at Francis and brought us to his room, sitting us on his bed. I repositioned myself to sit on top of his lap. I set my head on his shoulder, his arms still around my waist. We sat like that for a while and I ended up falling asleep. When I awoke he was behind me, his arms around me tightly.

"Good morning, beautiful." He kissed around my ear and then slowly down my jaw.

"You sure are eager today." I pointed out. He stopped, looking at me.

"Because it's your birthday… I have to be."

"Ugh, don't remind me." I groaned. He continued kissing my jaw and cheeks, but I turned my head so he kissed me on the lips.

"Your birth needs to be celebrated, love."

"No, it doesn't. I'm older than you… *that* doesn't need to be celebrated."

"Carmen… I'm 304."

"So I'm dating an old man?" We laughed and I kissed him again.

"You're going to want to call your mom." I groaned and sat up. I reached for my phone and called Mom.

Nine

"Happy birthday, Carmen!" I turned the ph-one on speaker after Felix heard what she said.

"Thanks, Mom. How are you?"

"I'm alright. Are you going to come home to get ready?" She asked as she bit her lip.

"Possibly,"

"You better take some cute photos of yourself."

"Don't worry, I will." I smiled.

"Okay, I love you, Carmen."

"Love you too, Mom." I said, hanging up at the same time as her.

Felix grabbed my hips and placed me on top of him. My phone dinged and he stopped, letting me grab it. It was a bunch of different social media notifications that I didn't care to check.

"I suppose you should get ready." He wrapped his arms around me.

"None of my clothes are here, we gotta stop at my house." I looked up.

"Wear one of my shirts~" He cooed and placed a kiss on my neck.

"Fine, you choose." He smiled and walked us up to his closet. He let go of me and looked at his closet. He reached his hand out at a gray shirt with a small smiley face on the chest to the left. It looked two sizes too big for me, but I liked loose stuff, and he thought I looked cute in his shirts anyways.

"This, paired with some shorts, if you'd like." He smiled, handing me the shirt.

"This works," I pulled my shirt off and changed into his. I went through my bag and grabbed the pair of shorts I packed. After I was done changing Felix and I walked out to the living space.

"Happy birthday, Carmen!" Carly called out, running out of her bedroom and giving me a hug.

"Thanks, Carly." I smiled, hugging back.

"Happy birthday, Carmen." Francis smiled, handing me a small gift box. "It's from me and Alice, I hope you like it." I took it softly from his grasp and ripped the bow off carefully, opening the box to find a beautiful moonstone ring, shaped into a heart.

"Oh, I love it! Thank you, Francis!" I gave him a hug and spotted Alice across the room. I ran up and hugged her. "Thank you, Alice. It's perfect."

"Happy birthday, Carmen. I'm glad you like it." She smiled. Felix walked up to me and softly grabbed the ring from me, taking my right hand in his, and placing it on.

"It resembles you, it's beautiful." He smiled, kissing my hand lightly and releasing his light grip. I blushed a bright pink.

"You guys gotta get going to school." Francis reminded, "*All* of you. Or you'll *all* have to redo your senior year." He chuckled lightly and threw Felix his keys. Felix grabbed my arm in his and led us out to his car.

"How come my *parents* get to give you a birthday gift but I can't?"

"Isn't our love a gift in itself?" I smiled and placed a hand on top of his.

"I suppose, but I do have one gift that I've wanted to give you for a while now. If you'll accept it, of course." He returned my smile, repositioning our hands so he was grasping mine. He started the car and pulled out of the drive.

"I mean, I suppose I'll accept this *one* gift." He reached into his back pocket and pulled out a small box.

"Just be aware, there will be a lot more than this one gift in your lifetime, Carmen." I blushed and he handed me the small box.

I opened the lid carefully, undoing the red bow that was tied neatly around it. I peered inside to find a beautiful set of earrings and a matching necklace. The necklace was two rings intertwined. *Our* rings.

"I noticed you stopped wearing our promise ring recently, so I made a quick search around your room one night and found it. To make this. The earrings are made with the same gem that was in our rings, *moonstone*. Coincidentally, is also your birthstone, which also coincidentally, matches the ring Francis and Alice gifted to you. The earrings aren't heart-shaped like any of the gems in the rings are, though." He looked over at me and laughed at my blank expression.

"I love it, Felix. Thank you." I was at a loss for words.

The only reason *why* I didn't wear my promise ring was that I could have sworn I lost it. I hadn't been able to find it for weeks. I felt terrible losing a ring so expensive, so I hadn't told him. I felt bad that he assumed I just didn't want to wear it, because of course I did, it may or may not have been buried in my hamper, underneath my dirty laundry.

He laughed a low, calming laugh, "Yeah, I did have to dig through your laundry, but honestly, that reaction of yours makes it worth it. I know you didn't mean to lose the ring, it's not your fault, love." He looked over at me, placing a reassuring kiss on my hand.

We drove to school in silence. He rubbed the back of my hand and hummed along to the songs on the CD he pushed in. When we pulled up to school, he parked in his usual spot, the best spot, the spot closest to the front doors. A crowd of people rushed over and yelled 'Happy Birthday, Carmen!', making me flush and Felix laugh.

Felix walked us to class, his arm tight around my waist, protecting me from the crowd of people.

"Don't worry, love." He squeezed my side and walked into English. Ms. Rossum closed the door after shooing away the crowd.

"Happy Birthday, Carmen. Sorry about the crowd, people are just worried about you. It has only been two days since you got back." She smiled.

"It's alright, really." I returned her smile. Felix walked us to our desks and sat me down. The bell rang and people rushed in. Felix held my hand and lifted it to his lips, placing a soft kiss on my pale skin. Ms. Rossum was reading a book called *Wolf Hollow* and Felix and I talked.

"Carly is arranging a small party at our house." He squeezed my hand, "*Don't* worry, it's just your friends and my family-" He wanted to say more but he must have seen something. His eyes grew wider, and everything around us paused, frozen in place. The sudden stop in motion shocked me, but I didn't comment on it.

"Felix?... What is it?" He shook his head.

"Sorry, love... Just more information. I wasn't expecting any today."

"Tell me," I demanded.

"Can't this wait?" His slight anger shocked me. A sudden red rose appeared in his hand. I jumped, startled as he handed it to me.

"W-" I started, but he cut me off.

"I guess they forgot to tell you," He paused, his expression blank. "Us immortals can manifest and make things." He didn't have to whisper as everything around us was frozen in place. "And since I control minds, I can also make this happen." He gestured a hand around the place.

"Why didn't they tell me?" I muttered.

"I guess it just skipped over their heads. They don't do it as much as I do." He manifested a full soda can in front of me and one in front of himself.

I took a sip and looked at him. "Why don't you do this more often?"

"Oh trust me, I do this all the time. And now that you know, I can do it more." Another red rose appeared in his hand.

"Why do you keep sending roses?" I cocked my head.

"Symbol of love. And I send them as an apology, in this case, it's an apology for my tone and choice of words. And the fact that I've never told you this before." He handed the rose to me. Luckily, he manifested ones with no thorns on them, so I didn't have to worry about that.

"Is there anything you *can't* do?" He laughed although it was a serious question. He read my mind, realizing I meant it seriously.

"Yeah, I can't leave you. And I'm not good at love… " I blushed.

"You know that's not what I mean." I smiled, referring to the 'I can't leave you' part. He wrapped an arm around my waist again.

"Give me one second," He looked off into the distance and then back at me. "After I unfreeze them, there will be two early dismissal passes 'from Francis' and I'm going to take you somewhere."

"Felix… No… We can't skip school." He held a hand to my cheek.

"You're fine, it's your birthday. And I'm going to take you somewhere nice." He placed a soft kiss on my cheek and rubbed my hand. He closed his eyes and suddenly everything around us was playing again. A girl walked in and had two green passes in her hands. She handed the passes to Ms. Rossum and left the room.

"Felix, Carmen, someone is here to pick you up." Her gaze met mine and Felix grabbed my hand, pulling me up to leave. We grabbed the passes from her, said goodbye, and left the classroom.

"Where are we-"

"Shh. It's a surprise." He walked us out to his maroon Volvo and opened my door, flashing to the other side. "Music?" He climbed in and buckled, his hand reaching over the middle column as he started the engine. I nodded and pressed the *CD* button, playing my song.

"I love you." I smiled, leaning over to kiss him.

"I love *you*." He returned my smile and pulled out of his parking space.

We drove for close to fifteen minutes and I started noticing the scenery around us, it was familiar, not new. We passed by a bunch of beach houses.

"Felix… *Where* are we going?" I looked over at him.

"Private reservation. Gift from Alice." That's all he answered with, no information or explanation, just *that*. He kept driving, going over a gated bridge, and into a beautiful, tropical island, separated from the rest of the houses on the beaches we passed.

"This is where we will be staying until we leave Haines. We will go to my house for the party tomorrow, and come back here until graduation."

"Felix-" I was at a loss for words. All I could do was gape at the beautiful island before us.

He smiled and squeezed my hand. He pulled into the driveway and flashed around to open my door. Instead of just letting me get up, he took me into his arms, bridal style, and walked me to the massive, french front doors. We walked inside and there were red roses *everywhere*. There were vases full of them, paintings of them, and even a red rose pillow on the white couch in the foyer.

"*This is* where we will be staying until we leave, Ms. Brooks." I blushed at what he called me and he smiled, walked me into the living room, setting me down on the couch as he sat himself down beside me.

"I-I-" I tried to speak but Felix cut me off, connecting our lips together. When we pulled away he grabbed my hand and pulled me up the stairs.

"Our room is up here." He explained as he opened another large set of French doors.

The room was *huge*. It had an amazing view of the beach, a nice, large canopy bed, a TV, a dresser, a walk-in closet, and literally *everything* anyone could wish for in a room.

"I hope you're happy." He smiled, leaning our foreheads together.

"Of course, I am. How could I *not* be?" I leaned my head up a little bit to push our lips together.

"You're pretty hard to please." He laughed.

"I am not," I breathed out, smiling back at him.

"Want to go swimming?" He asked, getting off of me.

He manifested himself in a pair of swim trunks. I gaped, at both his body, and me still not being used to his manifesting. He laughed, and manifested *me* a black bikini, but changed it out for a one-piece, thinking I was uncomfortable.

"No," I stretched the word and protested, making him change my swimsuit back to that black bikini. He grabbed me up by my waist and pulled me close to him. "I'm trying to become more comfortable, especially around you." I blushed, standing on my tippy-toes and kissing his cheek.

"I'm proud of you."

He smiled, taking my hand and leading me out to the balcony that overlooked the inlet that surrounded Haines.

The balcony had a hot tub on it, along with string lights, a projector, and a small little drinks stand of lemonade.

"Hot tub, or open water?" He looked at me, cocking his head.

"Hot tub, I don't understand how people can swim in Alaska's waters, even in June it's freezing cold." He laughed.

"Oh wait... This place *does* have a pool. It may be cold, but I could change the temperature." I nodded and he walked us outside.

"I don't understand why you're doing all of this." He stopped walking and looked down at me.

"Carmen, it's your birthday, love. I'm doing this because I love you." I blushed and he kept walking. When we got to the pool he dipped his foot in and shrugged. "I'm not the best at telling temperatures, if you need me to change it I can." He gestured for me to try out the water, so I stuck my foot in and shrugged as well.

"It's not *that* cold." I smiled, letting go of his hand and jumping in.

"Carmen!" He laughed, jumping in after me.

His dirty blond hair looked almost as dark as Alice's. His hands drifted up to smooth out my light blonde hair, and mine drifted down to his chest, outlining his abs.

"You're beautiful," He told me, leaning in and closing the space between our lips. "You're the most gorgeous thing I've ever laid my eyes on, Carmen. I can *promise* you that." I blushed, obviously.

"Felix... Will you tell me your story? Please?" I leaned my forehead against his, worried he would get upset.

"Let's move this conversation to the hot tub, shall we?" I nodded.

He walked us over to the hot tub, pressed the jet button, set it to low, and sat us in the hot tub, me on his lap. He exhaled hard before he spoke.

Ten

"*1718...* I was dying of the Plague... Francis was, and is, a doctor, and I was, and am, his son, so he saved me. He made me drink the elixir, our red drink, and saved me. He couldn't bare to lose his one and only family, so he made me and the rest of my family immortal. The same situation happened with Carly, Seth, and Josh." He paused, his face cold, and sad.

"Felix... You don't have to..." He locked our lips together, making me forget what I was about to protest.

"I don't mind talking about it. Really." He set his forehead to mine and his arms tightened around my waist as he exhaled. He continued speaking, rubbing my hand as if *I* needed comfort.

"Carly, Seth, and Josh were all dying of the Spanish flu as well. Francis and Alice turned me immortal a couple of days before them, seeing how I would handle it, and if they would get caught." He paused, searching in his mind. "Eventually I learned to accept it, but in my first year of being an immortal, I couldn't stop drinking the elixir, I was addicted. About a year after I got used to eating and drinking normal things." He clicked his tongue.

"How often do you have to drink the elixir?"

"At least a sip every month, otherwise the effects can decrease." He clicked his tongue again, "Not much, but still."

"What's even in the elixir?" His face turned cold, and I looked down at my hands, knowing he didn't want to explain.

"I-" He began.

"You don't need to explain… I'm-" He placed a hand under my chin, making me look up at him.

"Carmen… It's alright. Really. Just when I tell you don't think of me as disgusting." He chuckled, "The elixir consists of human and animal blood, normally from people and animals who were dying or… since

Francis is a doctor, some from blood tests and such. Special herbs, and all sorts of things." He looked down at the water.

"You're not disgusting." I looked up at him, "As you said, it's blood from people that are dying or from blood tests, it's not like you *kill* people… right?" He didn't say anything and that spoke volumes.

"I…" He paused, "Back when I was addicted to the elixir… I *did* kill a few people… But please don't think of me differently, love. That was 300 years ago, and after a sip of the human blood in the drink it can make you go crazy-" He rambled on but I made him stop by placing my lips to his again. He kissed back and his hands moved to my hips, pulling me closer.

"I don't think you're a monster and I don't think of you differently. I think of you as the amazing, caring, boyfriend that you are. Okay?" *He* blushed, for the first time literally ever, and smiled.

"Okay," He mumbled softly, moving his lips to my jaw, and kissing along it. Changing my mind from the fact he blushed to the fact that *I'm* blushing. He smiled, hearing my thoughts, and continued kissing me.

"I love you," I breathed out as we pulled away for a second.

"I love *you*,"

Felix and I were lying in bed, 'watching' TV. He had turned on some comedy show I didn't care to pay attention to, as I was comfortable laying my head on his lap, and him having an arm around me, rubbing my side. He laughed at the TV a couple of times, and then apologized, even though I told him it was alright and I didn't mind. After about an hour of that, I looked over at the clock and gaped.

"Eleven o'clock already?"

"Wow. Why don't you go get changed, I'll meet you in the bathroom." He smiled, sitting up as I walked into the closet full of stuff he manifested for me before we got here. I picked out a royal blue lace nightgown and walked back out to the bedroom.

"You look *beautiful*," His eyes went wide and he flashed over to me, wrapping his arms around my waist and leaning down. I blushed and he kissed me, one of his hands roaming up my back and to my jaw, holding it soft, yet strong.

"I need to wash my face," I leaned away, slowly walking to the bathroom.

"Okay~" He whined, following me. I opened the mirror cabinet and pulled out my acne face wash, and my toothpaste.

I applied the facewash and brushed my teeth as I waited to wash it off. Felix didn't need to brush his teeth or wash his face, because being an immortal basically means that you're perfect, just like he is. Just like I *wish* I could be. He frowned at my thoughts,

"Love, you *are* perfect. Your imperfections aren't imperfections to anyone but yourself. You're beautiful, cute, and loving. Your slight acne and the color of your teeth don't change that."

He wrapped an arm around my waist, standing by my side, looking at my body as I looked at him in the mirror. I finished brushing my teeth and washed my face, patting the water off with a white towel Felix handed me. He picked me up after I set the towel down and walked me over to the bed.

"I have legs," I laughed, yet snuggling into his warm chest. He set me on the bed, climbing in next to me and moving a blanket over both of us. He turned the TV on some relaxing music.

I set my head on his chest and stretched my leg over his. His right arm traveled behind my back and settled on my hand that lay on his chest.

"Goodnight, love. Happy birthday, I love you." He kissed the top of my head and smiled.

"Night, Felix. I love *you*." I snuggled into his chest more. I fell asleep shortly after and when I awoke, Felix wasn't laying next to me.

I rolled my legs over the side of the bed and found a neatly written note on the bedside table, with my name printed perfectly. The note, written in old-fashioned cursive, read;

Carmen,

I went out to go grab some more elixir from Francis.

I hope to be back before you awake, but if not, I'll be back shortly. Don't worry.

Love, Felix

I put the note back on the bedside table, put my phone in my pocket, and walked downstairs to the kitchen. I grabbed a couple of waffles out of the freezer and popped them in the toaster, and I checked the notifications I didn't care to check yesterday.

There were one-thousand, three-hundred, forty-nine notifications across all of my social media apps. Most of them consisted of happy birthday DMs, posts, and comments. Other notifications were likes and comments on Carly, Harley, Jenny, and Mom's posts *about* my birthday.

Carly texted me the information about the birthday party being tonight at four, and that Felix was almost here. I thanked her and then went to the living room to eat my waffles. I was watching some prison documentary as Felix unlocked and walked in the front door.

"Hey," He leaned up against the door frame and smiled and I ran up to him after he set the bottles of elixir down. "I love you, too." He laughed, hugging me tightly.

"How long have you been gone?" I looked up at him.

"An hour, maybe less." I stood on my tippy-toes to kiss him and his arms stayed wrapped around my waist tightly. "I wasn't even gone for that long. Did you just miss me that much?" He teased, lifting me up in his arms and setting me down on the couch.

"Yes." I climbed on top of his lap and set my head on his chest, listening to his breathing and imagining his heartbeat.

The coffee pot beeped and he lifted me up, still clenched to his chest, and walked over to the kitchen. He set me down and got out a coffee cup, pouring some coffee into it. I walked over to the giant fridge and grabbed my creamer. I handed it to him and he poured the perfect amount into my coffee and put the creamer back.

"Thank you," I kissed his cheek and picked my coffee up, bringing it to our room with me. He followed, closing our door behind him.

"Finish your coffee and then take a shower. We're going to go somewhere special." He smiled and I nodded, sipping my hot coffee and walking over to the computer that sat on the big, clear desk.

I sat down and placed my coffee on a coaster sitting on the desk. Felix opened the giant blinds overlooking the inlet. He stood there and exhaled hard.

"Felix? What's wrong?" I stood up and walked over to him, grabbing his hand.

"It's nothing, love." He turned to face me, putting on a fake smile. "Really, I'm alright."

He leaned down and placed a kiss on my cheek, and then faced to walk out of the room. I followed, not believing that everything was okay.

"Carmen. I'm okay, you have no need to follow me. I'm just going to put the elixir in the fridge, okay?" I nodded and watched as he walked out of our room, closing the door. I walked back to the desk and sat down. Carly texted me, and what she sent worried me.

'Felix *isn't* okay.' she sent.

'How so?'

'I can't explain. But just keep him comforted, safe, and busy.'

'He's kind of angry with me right now, but I'll try.'

'Why is he angry?'

'I asked if he was okay and then got a little protective.'

'Alright, well just keep him company, and don't get upset with him.'

'Okay, thank you, Carly.'

'No problem. Bye, Carmen.'

Felix walked in and leaned against the doorway, a cold, serious look on his face. "Who were you texting?"

"Carly... What's wrong?"

"Nothing." He muttered, closing the door and walking over to me. "Nothing is wrong. Is there something wrong with you? You okay?" His arm snaked around my waist, pulling me close.

"Yeah, I'm fine. You just seem... off..." I pushed him back onto the bed, me hovering over top of him.

"Carmen..." He murmured.

"Yeah yeah, I know. 'No more.'" I came off ruder than I expected and I climbed off of him, going over to the window. "Sorry..." I muttered. "I'm not trying to push you into doing anything."

"I know. It's okay, I'd be annoyed too, it's just… I'm not good at love, and you're the first person I've grown attached to, and… I want to do it right." He walked up behind me, snaking an arm around my waist.

"I know…"

He put his hand under my chin, turning my head to look at him

"I have no reason to be upset… I'm with you, the prettiest, most gorgeous thing I've ever laid my eyes on. The sun to my dark life." He tilted his head, placing a soft, yet passionate kiss on my lips.

"I love you, *forever.*" I blushed and smiled, looking up at him.

"I love *you, forever.*" He returned my smile and let go of my waist, walking over to the computer, my hand in his.

He sat me down and stood behind me, watching me type out a school document. The document is about our experience in senior year and our overall view of being a student. I was almost done with the two-thousand-word essay we had to work on, but it could very much use a tune-up… Or an editor.

"I could edit it for you if you'd like." Felix read my thoughts and smiled, turning the office chair I sat in to face him.

"It's alright. I'd rather you spend your free time on me." I smiled, jumping into his arms, and instantly snuggling into his chest. My phone rang and Felix answered it.

"Hey," He answered, holding a finger up to my mouth as I mouthed the words 'Who is it?'

"Mhm… Yeah, give me just one second." He sat down on the bed, me still on his lap, and handed me the phone.

"Hello?"

"Carmen? Are you alright? I didn't see you at home when I went to pick you up. Where are you?"

"Oh, sorry Jenny, I must've not told you. Felix brought me to a house that was a gift from Ali… His mother. I'll see you in a little bit."

"Alright, see you at school." She hung up and I looked at Felix.

I got up off of his lap and walked over to the closet, taking off the blue lace nightgown I still had on and switching it to a pair of light blue ripped jeans, and a sage green tank top. When I walked out he had manifested himself in a pair of black sweatpants and a plain gray t-shirt.

"Don't worry, we have time." He walked up to me, placing his arms around my waist and closing his eyes.

When he opened his eyes he smiled, walking me over to the mirror. He had manifested my classical makeup look. He turned my head to look up at him and then kissed me, making me blush a bright pink instantly.

"Breakfast?" He grabbed my hand and walked me out of our room.

"We don't have enough time." I followed him and he walked to the foyer, picking up our backpacks and his keys. He handed me my dark green messenger bag and I threw it over my shoulder.

"If we don't have enough time for breakfast then I think we best get going." He held my hand again and walked outside, turning around to lock the door, and then heading to the car.

He opened my door for me and then flashed over to the driver's side, getting in at the same time as me. He drove us to school and manifested a coffee for me as he pulled into his parking spot, the best one in the lot, the one most people fight over, the one that takes years to get just one day parked in, all reserved for us.

"*Now* I see what you meant by 'I'm going to be doing it a lot more'." I smiled, taking my drink from him. He laughed, looking over at me.

"I told you." He smiled, leaning over the middle column to kiss me.

When we got out he flashed over to me and took my hand in his. Alex came racing up to us.

"Carmen! I just wanted to ask if you and Felix wanted to see the play that Miles and I are doing Saturday." He smiled and tried to steady his breathing.

"Um…" I looked over to Felix. 'Are we going to be in town Saturday?' I thought, knowing he would hear it and send me some kind of sign. He nodded and smiled.

"Yeah, Felix and I will still be in town then, so I think we could make it." I smiled as Alex jumped up and down.

"Thank you, thank you!" He hugged me but pulled away quickly. "What do you mean 'Felix and I will *still* be in town'?" He cocked his head.

"Oh, we must have not told you, I thought we did… Uhm, Felix and I are going to Fairbanks for college." I looked down at my hands and Felix rubbed my hand, trying to comfort me.

"Oh… Well, we don't have to worry!" He got rid of his saddened expression, "I'm taking the acting and film classes in Fairbanks! It's just a building a little separated from yours, but we'll still be together!" He smiled, hugging me yet *again*.

"That's great!" I returned his smile, "Have you found out what colleges Harley and Jenny are going to?"

"Jenny, yes, Harley, not sure. Jenny is going to Anchorage, and I think Harley is too, but I'm not sure. Miles is going to Fairbanks too, he's taking the acting classes because he loves acting and because I'm the love of his life." He snickered. "Michael is going to Anchorage 'cause of Jenny." He added, "That's all I've heard, though. Class is about to start and Miles is waiting for me so I gotta bounce. I'll see you at lunch?" He ran off to the gates before I could say goodbye.

"And you say *I* know everything." Felix snickered.

"Technically you *do*." I shot back, smiling at him.

We walked to class together and Mrs. Gearey welcomed us and told us to sit wherever. We had some science videos on, and for the entirety of all of them, Felix and I talked. He talked about how beautiful I was, and I talked about the party.

The day went by pretty fast. The slowest part was gym, obviously. It was dodgeball, and since Felix is good at everything, he played, leaving me to stand in the corner talking to Miles and Alex. They flirted a lot, but we had an interesting conversation about what the play they were in was about, and then Alex bragged about being the lead.

After school was over Felix drove us to our house for the next week, and told me to get ready for the party. I slipped on the light blue dress Alice had picked out for me and gave to me for my birthday, and put on the necklace Felix gave me, along with the earrings and the ring that Francis and Alice had gifted me. I walked out and Felix immediately came up to me.

"You look *stunning*." He snaked an arm around my waist and smiled, leaning down to place a gentle kiss on my lips.

"You look amazing yourself." I looked him up and down, smiling at the black suit and white dress shirt he wore. He had a light blue tie that matched my dress. He looked over at the clock.

"It's 4:50. We best get going." He held my hand and walked me out to the car, opening my door, letting me get in, and closing it, flashing over to the driver's side.

When we arrived Carly ran out of the house and hugged me as soon as Felix opened my door.

"Happy Birthday... Party!" She smiled and Felix snickered, shaking his head slightly.

"Thanks," I smiled back at her. Although I could care less about birthdays, it makes me happy knowing that other people can make them seem joyful. If I didn't have people like Alice, Carly, or Jenny around, I probably wouldn't even celebrate.

"C'mon, let's go inside." She grabbed my hand and pulled me up the stairs to their house.

When we entered, Felix's family was there, along with Jenny, Miles, Michael, Harley, and Alex. When we came within sight, they all yelled

"Happy birthday, Carmen!" I blushed, surprised by the gesture, and how many people showed up.

"Don't worry, no one else is coming," Felix whispered, taking my hand in his, 'helping' me down the three steps to the living room.

"We hope it's not too much," Alice smiled, "When Carly has something in mind it's hard to say no." Francis and Alice chucked.

"I *love* your dress, Carmen!" Jenny came up to me, Harley following close behind. "I didn't know you were really into dresses. I thought it was jeans, t-shirts, and sweatshirts." She laughed, trying to make a joke out of my usual, 'before Felix and Carly took over' outfits.

"Well, now that *I'm* here, her outfits will be dresses and gowns." Carly smiled, putting an arm around my shoulders.

"How about we have a party?" Francis smiled, seeing as I was slightly uncomfortable with them judging my outfits.

Everyone nodded and then gathered in small groups to talk, listening to the music. Felix, Carly, Alex, and I all gathered to talk. Alex asked Carly if she'd like to go to Miles and his' play Saturday and she said yes, smiling at him as he ran off to Jenny and Harley.

Carly walked off, saying she would leave us be. Felix put an arm around my waist and held my other hand high in his. He lifted me up a little and set my feet on his so I was just a couple of inches shorter than him.

He swayed us back and forth, not dancing too much, but since I can't dance, this sufficed. He smiled, noticing my blush as Francis, Alice, Carly, Jenny, and Harley watched. Miles and Alex started dancing together and were laughing when they messed up.

Carly got out the camera I brought and started recording Felix and me dancing. She panned over to Miles and Alex a couple of times, but mainly focused the camera on us.

Eleven

"I hope you had fun," Felix kissed my jaw, sending shivers down my spine.

"I did, thank you." I smiled as he moved his lips from my jaw to my cheek, to my neck. Sending waves of happiness down my body.

"I'm glad," He smiled against my skin. He stopped and looked at me. "Want to go home? Or stay here?" He smiled, trying to sit up.

"I wouldn't mind going home," I sat my body up just enough to latch our lips together and pull him down, he still hovered over my body.

"Alright, let's go." He pulled away and sat up, taking my hand and pulling me up, too.

We walked out of his room and then said goodbye to Francis and Alice. We walked out of the house and to his car. He opened my door for me and then raced around to the other side.

"Y'know you don't have to do that. I think I know how to open a door." I laughed and so did he, knowing I was talking sarcastically. He pressed the CD button and then took my hand in his. Pulling out of the drive he started a conversation.

"Oh, I forgot to tell you. Your mom knows about the house we are staying at. That's why she hasn't called asking where you were. She knows that we will be staying here, and she said that's fine." He smiled.

"Okay," I muttered, looking out the window.

"Something wrong?"

"No… It's just… I can't believe that graduation is in 2 days, and I'm already 18…" He cut me off.

"Carmen, I'm older than you… I'm 304, remember?" He smiled an even brighter smile.

"Oh yeah, how could I forget I'm dating an old man?" I looked at him, smiling without even knowing it.

"I love you," He turned back to face the road.

"I love *you*," I was looking at him, still leaning over the middle column.

We arrived at the house twenty minutes later, and he flashed over to open my door, not caring that I can do it myself. He walked with my hand in his, bringing us into the house. He immediately brought us upstairs after locking the front door. He sat on the bed and I sat next to him. He put a hand under my chin and moved our faces in a way that made them search for each other's lips.

After we disconnected I got up to go get ready for bed, he followed behind when I went into the bathroom.

I brushed my teeth and washed my face, looking up at him after I put on chapstick. He leaned down and kissed my forehead, smiling against my skin. I walked over to the closet and changed into a silk, yellow-lace nightgown. It was almost the same as the one I wore last night, just more *revealing* than I'd thought. I walked out and Felix wasn't in our room. I searched upstairs and then heard talking coming from the living room. I walked down and saw Felix pacing around, talking on the phone.

"Hey," I peered around the corner and his attention shifted to me. His upset gaze turned loving in an instant.

"One second, Francis." He muted his phone as I walked up to him.

"Everything alright?" I wrapped my arms around his neck, standing on my tippy-toes.

"Yeah…" He smiled, trying to hide what was happening.

"Tell me," I looked down, "Please," I added and he chuckled.

"Fine. But only because you are too cute when you demand things thinking I'll be angry." He put his phone to his ear again. "Francis, I'll call you back in a little bit." He nodded once and hung up the phone.

He moved us to the couch and sat down beside me. I put my head on his lap facing the ceiling and he started smoothing out my hair. "Francis said some immortals in the area won't leave us alone because of the elixir… They tried breaking in but Josh was home and shooed them off." He paused, and I looked up at him.

"It'll be alright," I tried to comfort him, but he shook his head.

"It won't be alright if they smell you. Your blood… I mean… They're newer immortals, and two of the three are still addicted to their elixir. All magical elixirs, whether they are immortal drinks, love potions, etcetera, are made with human and animal blood. Depending on how much blood was used in the elixir, depends on how much the drinker will be affected. For us, it's about a year, on the other hand, Floyd's clan and their elixir can make that thirst last for *centuries.*"

His hand moved from my hair to my cheek, rubbing it with his thumb, making me grow redder by the second. His face was blank, his mind elsewhere.

"Felix?..." I sat up a little but he set me back down with a hand on my stomach. I remembered I was wearing that thin, yellow lace nightgown that showed off my stomach area because of the semi-see-through fabric that was used.

"I don't want to make you stay up all night explaining something that can be taken care of in a day." He removed his hand from my stomach but I wished he kept it there. He sat me up and I leaned on his shoulder.

"How about we go to sleep?" He smiled, looking down at me as I looked up at him. I nodded and he helped me up, holding my hand in his as he walked us up the stairs.

"Did I ever tell you how beautiful you are?" I blushed and he laid me down on the bed, laying next to me. I snuggled into his chest and his arms wrapped around my back, turning himself over so I was on top of him.

"I love you," I whispered, yawning after I said it.

"I love you, too." He whispered back, smiling as I yawned again. "Okay, it's time to sleep."

"Okay. Goodnight," I snuggled into his chest and he rubbed my back with one hand, creating friction with my skin, the lace, and the silk.

After I fell asleep it felt like seconds until I woke up again. I was still on top of Felix, and he was still rubbing my back, but it felt… strange.

"Felix…" I muttered into his shirt.

"Hmm?" He placed a kiss on my head.

"What time is it?" I blushed, happy he couldn't see.

"Uhm… 11:51, any particular reason why?"

"Last night just felt so fast. It felt like I was asleep for only a minute." I pushed my head harder into his chest.

"Huh, weird." He moved his hands from my back down to my waist.

"Oh crap, it's the 4th isn't it?" I sat up as he did too.

"I'll go and make breakfast, you get ready." He climbed off the bed and walked downstairs, manifesting a new outfit before he was fully out of sight.

I went over to the walk-in closet and went to the translucent bag, hanging up behind my other dresses. I pulled the royal blue, knee-length dress out of its bag and slipped off my lace nightgown, pulling the dress on and looking in the tall mirror to zip it up. I grabbed my silver shoes and walked out of the closet. I put on my usual makeup but added matching blue eyeshadow and used liquid eyeliner instead. I walked down the stairs, holding my shoes in one hand and my silver crossbody purse in the other. Felix was wearing a black suit with a white undershirt, similar to the outfit he wore to my birthday, just not as loose. I peeked around the hallway door and he turned his attention to me.

"You look *stunning*." He smiled, leaving the eggs he was making and flashing over to me, setting his hands around my waist.

"*You* look stunning." I returned his smile, wrapping my arms around his neck as I set my stuff on the counter nearby.

"Breakfast?" He released his slight grip on me, walking over to the food he was making. I nodded and he got out a plate and a coffee cup. I sat down on the bright yellow breakfast bar stools and Felix dished up my plate.

"It always feels rude to eat when you don't." He set my plate down and extended his arms out, setting his hands on the edge of the counter.

"Well, I don't need to eat."

"I know… It just feels rude of me to just eat and you stand there."

"Would you rather I *pretend* to eat or just leave you alone to eat?" He rubbed my hand.

"Neither. It's just the human in me talking." I smiled, picking up my coffee cup and taking a sip. "Thank you. You really didn't have to do all of this." He smiled.

"I know. But you deserve it all." He placed a soft kiss on my lips. After I finished eating and then Felix took my arm, bringing me out of the house and into the car. When we got there Felix hooked our arms and walked into the school for the before party.

"Carmen!" Alex and Miles ran up to us, both of them dressed in their black graduation gowns and black and yellow caps. Alex gave me a hug while Miles nodded, causing Alex to push Miles closer to me, making us hug.

"I'm so excited for you guys' play tomorrow!" I smiled brightly after we disconnected, looking up at Felix for a second.

"Are you both coming?" Miles asked, not having heard from Alex.

"Wouldn't miss it." Felix smiled, moving his arm around my waist instead of being interlocked with mine.

"Yay! We'll see you there then." Miles smiled, putting his arm around Alex. "Let's go get some punch." Alex and Miles skipped over to the snacks bar, filling up two clear cups with the red punch.

"The graduation ceremony is happening soon, let's go get our gowns on." Felix smiled, his arm tightening around my waist.

"Okay," I looked up at him, his face focused. "Is everything alright?" I asked, causing him to stop walking.

"Yeah… I'm alright." He kept walking and shook his head, changing his face from worried, back to happy.

We walked to the dressing rooms and grabbed our gowns with our names on the clear bags. Whoever paid had paid extra for our gowns, as our names were embroidered on the front underneath a red rose.

"I added the rose," Felix whispered, kissing my cheek. "Only on yours. Mine has an outline of a heart." He smiled, walking into the dressing room across from me.

I slid the gown over my dress and adjusted everything. My dress was just short enough to not show under the gown. I set the cap on my head, adjusting the way it sat on my head. When I walked out of the dressing room Felix took my arm and walked over to the corner of the room.

"Carly made sure to remind you there was a party tonight by sending me twenty-seven telepathic messages." He chuckled, placing a hand under my chin. "It'll be fine. It's just graduation, it's nothing to worry about." He smiled a bright white smile, placing a kiss on my lips, and basically making the world pause.

"I know..." I set my forehead against his after a good amount of kissing. "It's just... I don't know if I'm ready to leave Haines yet..." I looked down, our foreheads still connected.

"It'll be okay, " He placed a gentle kiss on my cheek and rushed us over to the group of graduates.

The graduation ceremony was what you'd expect. A speech was made by Carly and Michael, we got our names called and our diplomas handed, and a very strong handshake with the principal.

My parents were there and clapped while being the only people that entire day to give a standing ovation. I flushed just seeing them do that, but Felix said it was cute. After Felix and his family went, the graduation ceremony was over, parents went home, and everyone was getting ready for Carly's big graduation party, excited as no one but my friends and I had been there.

There were talks of the party and how exciting it would be because Francis and Alice were really chill and were 'probably popular in school' Felix told me people's thoughts surrounding the party and we laughed about it. Carly asked us to leave the ceremony early to help set up the last couple of things for the party.

Felix and Carly took control in putting away any sign of the fact they weren't normal humans, like locking up Francis's 'history room' that is full of old paintings, furniture, and decor from his past 800 years. I was instructed to get out some punch, and snacks, and to make sure the wine and elixir were hidden. The first guests arrived at around seven-twenty, although the party started at eight.

"We're lucky we can sense when people come." Felix laughed with Carly, who was smiling and still in her purple graduation dress.

"Carmen, if you would like, there is a dress more suitable for partying on Felix's bed. I manifested it for you, so it's one of a kind." She welcomed the first guests, which was followed by half of the school. Felix and I scurried off to his room, closing the door behind us.

"Get changed and then we gotta go be good hosts." He smiled, taking his phone out of his pocket and calling Francis.

I did as he said and got changed, slipping my royal blue graduation dress off and slipping on the bright yellow dress Carly manifested for me. I overheard some of Francis and Felix's conversation, but from what I can tell, was just more information on the immortals who are trying to break in. He pocketed his phone and looked over at me, fully dressed, just no shoes.

"You look amazing," He walked up to me, picked me up, and laid me on the bed, planting kisses all along my cheeks, jaw, and neck.

"She forgot shoes," I snickered, my body warming up by just his kisses.

"I think that was intentional." He smiled against my skin, basically trying to tell me that I was bad at wearing high heels. "Don't worry, I like having to make you stand on your tippy-toes just to reach me." He looked up, hearing my thoughts. "Really, I do. Just because you have a bad balance doesn't mean I don't love you."

He sat himself down on the bed, sitting me up. But little did he know, my 'sadness' was just a ploy to sit on his lap. I sent kisses down *his* neck and he chuckled, grabbing my waist as he fell back on the bed.

"Okay, we've really got to get out there." He smiled, standing up as I wrapped my legs around his waist and my arms around his neck.

"Okay~" I groaned but cooperated.

He walked us out of the room and downstairs into the 'party zone', since no one was allowed on any floor but the main floor. He set me down, holding my hand in the air, and spinning me around, spinning my hand above me. I blushed and he smiled, wrapping one of his arms around my waist and lifting me up a slight bit to set my now white dress-slippered feet on top of his. We danced for a while and then Alex and Miles came up to us.

"I can't believe you two are leaving Monday. We aren't leaving till the *middle* of the summer because what's the rush in moving?"

"We just thought it'd be nice to get a fresh start this summer and use up the majority of it making new memories in a new town, you know?" Felix smiled.

*The rush is big, Alex, like super duper we might **die to** rush, that's why we are moving a couple of days after school ends to maybe factor that risk of dying down.* I thought, and Felix looked at me, his smile decreasing slightly.

"I understand what you're getting at. Do you guys want some punch?" He changed the subject and Felix and I both nodded, following behind.

"I've got to go take this call, I'll be right back." Felix looked down at his phone. Before he walked off he rubbed my arm.

I reached into the drinks fridge and grabbed the punch. Carly had changed the bowl I put it in for a glass container with a spout built in. I poured a cup for myself and gestured toward them, asking if they wanted a glass.

"No thanks, we already have some." They held up their red solo cups and smiled.

I put the punch back and waited for Felix. I took a sip and the punch tasted bitter, although I just assumed that was because I don't drink punch much. Felix came back and smiled, walking up to me, and leaning against the counter.

"Hey pretty lady, can I buy you a drink?" He joked, making me laugh.

"Uhm, no thanks... I'm kind of waiting for my amazing, caring, hot boyfriend to show up. He had to take a call." I smiled, chugging the punch. The rest of the party went by pretty quickly, it was just a bunch of dancing and talking like most parties are.

The last group of people left around one-fourteen, and Felix instantly brought me to his bedroom, manifesting me in a nightgown similar to the ones I'd worn the past two nights, just black this time.

"Like always, you look great." He pushed me back onto the bed, making a trail of kisses down from my forehead to my collarbone. I blushed and he looked over at the clock. "I think you need to get some sleep." He whispered in my ear.

I nodded, moving over a little bit for him to lie down, and then shifting on my side. His arms wrapped around me instantly, and he started kissing my ear. We lay like that for a while and then I looked up at Felix.

"I'm really thirsty, could you get me some water?" I choked out, my throat dry. He nodded and sat up, manifesting a glass of water. I sat up in between his legs and took the water from him. I slugged it down as fast as I could and he manifested more.

"Slow down, love." He moved my hair from my face to behind my ear.

"I-I'm sorry… I'm just so thirsty." I managed to choke out in between gulps, still chugging the now infinite water Felix manifested.

"I think you should sleep, my love. It might pass in the morning." He put a hand on my thigh, rubbing it, trying to calm me down.

"I'm not tired, though. I feel super awake…" His eyes went wide.

"I'm calling Francis. Now." He scrambled to pick up his phone, calling Francis instantly.

"I know you know what I know. Get over here fast… Please."

"I'm coming," I heard Francis say. Felix hung up and picked me up, carrying me to the sitting room. When Francis got here I was asked a ton of questions. A lot of them I didn't understand why he was asking.

"What was the last thing you drank?"

"Uhm… I had some punch from the party, and water, just now."

"You're *not* tired, you said?" I nodded. "Can you show me where the punch is or was?" He asked very calmly, obviously trying not to make the situation worse.

My face was hot as I walked over to the drinks stand in the hallway to the kitchen, opened the mini-fridge, and pulled out the glass container which I had gotten the punch from. Felix's eyes went wide and both of them flashed over to me, taking the container from me.

"You don't think she…" Felix began, looking at Francis as he nodded.

"What? It's just some punch, there's nothing to…" I stopped, recalling the first time I had seen the White's 'punch' sitting on the counter in a similar container.

"Felix… go and lay with her, I'm going to retrieve Alice and we can do some *tests* in the morning." His face was overall calm, but his eyes explained his horror.

Felix brought me back to his room, laying me down on my side, his arms wrapped around me. I was crying. I was sorry. He hummed the tune of my song and tried to relax me, kissing my neck, and whispering 'It's okay,' from time to time.

"F… Felix… I'm so sorry," I sobbed and he shushed me.

"It's okay, love. It's okay." He cooed.

He tried calming me but his mind was still not set on the fact that I'd *drunk the elixir.* The magical potion that will make me stop aging, stop growing, and stop being *human*. He read my thoughts, manifesting a red rose and making my hands hold it.

"It's okay, we'll make it through this. I *promise.*"

He turned me around in his chest. I pushed my head into the space between his neck and shoulders, trying to collect my breathing, and at least *try* to quiet my sobs. We sat like that the most of the night, my crying eventually stopped, and he kept humming, trying to comfort me.

'What the hell are we going to tell her parents' Felix… said…?

"Did you say something, Felix?" I looked up at him.

"No, darling." He looked almost as scared as he did when Freya paralyzed him.

"I swear you just said something…" I put my head back into the crook of his neck and focused on my breathing.

"Then what happened to you is true…" He smoothed my hair, one of his arms tightly around me. He exhaled hard and calmed *his* breathing.

Twelve

When Alice eventually came home it was around six-thirty. Francis let Felix and I relax for a bit and then the testing began. We started with testing if I could receive a telepathic message from Felix. And if I could send one back.

'Hey, love.' He sent with a puzzled look on his face.

'Hi,' I replied, blushing.

"It worked!" Felix hugged me tightly.

"Felix…" Francis reminded, making Felix release me and clear his throat.

"What?" I asked, referring to why Felix couldn't be excited that it worked.

*'Francis is only saying that because he doesn't **want** you to be immortal, which makes sense, there was no **reason** for you to be an immortal. You were perfectly fine as a human.'* Felix sent, sending a mental image of a rose. *'Although, **I** find it okay... because I can do **that**."* He referred to the mental rose he sent, and honestly, I'm glad he *could* do that now.

"What else are we going to test?" I was still blushing from the things that Felix had sent.

"We could test manifesting, although it takes a while to figure out," Francis suggested as I tried picturing a rose in my hand. I focused on that and only that... Until Felix laughed.

"Darling, it takes a while to master." He smiled, manifesting a red rose and handing it to me in just mere seconds. I groaned, relaxing onto his shoulder. Alice walked back outside and handed me a bottle of the elixir.

"Put an unlimited spell on this for her, Felix. Please." She smiled at him and he closed his eyes for a minute.

"There," Felix returned her smile, watching as I drank the elixir nonstop, not having to take a breath.

"It's so weird," I began, breathing between sips although I didn't *have* to. "Not having to force myself to take a breath." I finished the sentence and the bottle, and it automatically refilled.

"That's just for drinking, you'll have to breathe, just like Felix does. Your heart just isn't pumping noticeably enough to hear." Francis corrected, seeing my sudden memories of listening to Felix's breath but not being able to hear his heartbeat.

"Okay," I didn't really listen as I was just chugging the elixir nonstop.

"Felix, stop her, she's going to over-drink," Alice told him, grabbing onto Francis' arm.

"It's alright, it's not going to do everything. You'd be doing the same if you'd just gone a night with that thirst." He mouthed a sorry after, probably for his tone. I heard what they were talking about and stopped drinking, handing the bottle to Felix. "Thank you," He smiled, holding the bottle by the cap and extending his arm down his leg.

"Felix, if you'd like you could try and teach her how to manifest. Start with something small." Francis nodded to him and walked off with Alice.

"Teach me~" I whined a couple of minutes after Francis and Alice left.

"Just… just one second, love." He concentrated his mind, manifesting an entire flower field of red roses. "I thought you'd want somewhere nice to practice. Somewhere that reminds you that I love you no matter what." He took my hand, dragging me to the amazing field of fresh, red, un-thorned roses.

"Felix…" I started, being cut off by a sudden desperate, yet loving, passionate kiss. I gasped, taken aback by his sudden affection.

"Shh, let's just relax for a little bit."

He pulled me down to the ground carefully, hovering over top of me, kissing my lips, cheeks, jaw, and neck, making my body shiver and my face flush a bright pink.

He moved down to my collarbone, lightly pressing his lips to it, sending a wave of pleasure throughout my entire body.

"That's so strange…" he breathed out in between kisses.

"What is?" I opened my eyes.

"Your heart… it's beating… How much of the elixir did you drink?"

"Only a solo cup full… why?" He sat up, pulling me in between his legs, and moving the hair that was out of place.

"Then it must just be the fact it was last night. As Francis said, your heart shouldn't be beating… at least not as noticeably as it is now."

"Should we talk to Francis?"

"I already sent a telepathic message… He just said to focus on manifesting and that we'll talk when they get back.

"You don't need to say 'Telepathic Message', I know what you mean." I sent a mental rose since I haven't been taught manifesting yet… Which we should get on.

"Hey! You did it!" He smiled, angling his head just right so he could kiss my upper cheek.

"I did!" I smiled back, flushing more at his excitement.

"Alright, we really *should* get on with the manifesting tests." He turned me in his lap so I was straddling him, "Close your eyes and picture an orange in front of you. You can see the texture of the peel, the bright orange color, and the small little stem at the top. You can smell the citrusy smell of it, and you can feel your finger running along the texture of the orange." He tried getting me to imagine the orange, but instead, I imagined *him*. When a small little version of him that could fit in the palm of my hand appeared, I opened my eyes and smiled.

"Carmen, love. This is *serious*." He tried to seem upset but smiled and laughed with me.

"You're better to imagine than an orange." I smiled back, leaning into his chest more as he smoothed my hair out.

"Seeing you blush over a mini-me is upsetting, I will admit." He crossed his arms around me, holding me tightly against his chest. He placed kisses over my jaw and neck, being satisfied when he saw the manifested version of himself fade and me blushing a very bright pink because of his affection.

"Okay, I should teach you *something*." He released his strong grasp on me, causing a shocking sensation to go through me. "Picture a red, *thornless* rose in your hand. Focus on the waxy feel of the petals on your fingers."

"Okay…" I closed my eyes, picturing a red rose. A couple of seconds later, a red rose appeared in my hand. "Ow-" I whined, forgetting to picture a rose *without* thorns.

"You okay?" Felix looked down at my hand and saw my wound close up. He made the thorns on the rose disappear.

"Yeah…" I looked back at my hand, seeing the wound was gone.

"Good. I'm glad the instant healing works." He smiled, taking the rose from my hand and setting it on the ground.

We practiced manifesting a bit more and then went to Francis. Felix taught me how to flash over somewhere as he had before and we had a race from the flower field to the house. He won, obviously, but I didn't care, I was just glad we would bond *this* way.

Francis said that we'd wait a couple of days and if my heartbeat is still noticeable, he can do some tests. Francis told us that we should go back to Felix and I's house, and just relax and explore my newfound powers.

When we arrived everything seemed brighter, more vivid, and more alive. Although, it may just be because I drank around a gallon of the elixir and the effects are very strong.

"That's how it looks in our eyes. You should look at yourself in a mirror." He smiled, taking my hand and walking to the front French doors.

"I thought you looked so much more alive when I saw you that night. I just thought someone spiked my drink maybe." I shrugged, walking with him into the foyer and taking off my shoes.

"Felix… The thirst is coming back…" I muttered, feeling ashamed that I was drinking so much.

"Here you go," He handed the bottle to me and then had a slightly upset look on his face.

"What?" I thought that his expression was 'cause of me drinking a lot.

"It's not that," He said, reading my thoughts. "Carmen, I've told you before that when you first drink the elixir a sort of thirst comes. You have no reason to be ashamed of 'drinking too much', love. I was like that, too."

He pulled me into the living room, sat us down on the bright yellow couch, and turned on the TV to some comedy show. I chugged the elixir until my throat said 'no more' to the bitter liquid. I set the bottle down on the clear coffee table that was in front of us.

'What the hell is Floyd going to think?' Felix thought, moving his hand to my thigh and rubbing his thumb against my skin, trying to distract himself.

"It'll be alright, " I assured him, speaking aloud instead of telepathically.

"Hm?" He stopped rubbing his thumb and cocked his head.

"Your thoughts. I-I was just responding to what you said about Floyd." I blushed, worried he would shield his thoughts or something to keep that from happening.

"I know," He put a finger under my chin, turning my head to look up at him. He set a soft and desperate, yet passionate kiss on my lips. I blushed brighter, molding our lips together again when he pulled away.

"Carmen..." He smiled and pulled away, "You're cute, but no." He continued rubbing his thumb across my skin, sending a tingling feeling through my body.

"What *was* that?" I set my hand on top of his, looking down at his hand and then back at his face.

"Energy current." He responded blankly, still rubbing my thigh.

"Could you explain?" I wrapped my hand around his thumb, making him stop.

"Sorry… " He tried moving his hand but I set it back down.

"Just don't rub. It stings…" I looked back down at our hands.

"Alright. And yeah, I can explain. Energy flows through *everything,* Carmen. Everything. Because some of your energy has been taken by your newfound 'powers', there isn't as much energy in certain parts of your body. Like your heart." He paused, moving his hand up to my chest, and placing it on my heart.

"Which is still beating very noticeably, I might add." He looked back at me, "Because you're an immortal now, you have the same amount of energy as me, and since you're so new to it, it'll feel weird for a while. Like you get a slight electrical shock."

"So this is normal for you? To *feel* energy?" He chuckled.

"Yes, not as bad as when you first get turned, but yes although it's technically just because we have active and good senses."

"How long will this last?" His hand was still on my chest and the energy transferring was driving me crazy.

"Probably a month or so. It'll only feel like this when you have contact with other immortals." He removed his hand, setting it back on my thigh as the energy transfer wasn't as bad in that spot.

Felix and I were laying in a newly manifested flower field around our house, me on top of him, trying my best to ignore the energy transfer. He had his arm wrapped tightly around my waist, rubbing my side. My head was buried in the crook of his neck, trying to control my thirst.

"Need more elixir?" He whispered and kissed my ear.

I shook my head, exhaling hard at just the mention of the elixir, and then nodded, giving in.

"Here, love." He handed me the clear water bottle with the currently unlimited red drink inside.

"Thanks,"

I sat up and set the bottle to my lips, closing my eyes and tilting my head back, taking one long swig of the red, bitter drink. I drank a lot and opened my eyes, taking the bottle away from my lips, and looking down at Felix. The bottle was instantly replaced with his lips, causing me to gasp and close my eyes again, relaxing into the kiss, and kissing back.

"I don't understand how you love me," He whispered, his forehead against mine.

"How could I not? You're amazing, talented, smart, and hot, if I may add." I leaned my head away from him, putting my hand on top of his. "I don't understand how you love *me*." He flinched at just my thought.

"I really think you need to look in the mirror. Carmen, you're gorgeous, brilliant, even before you became immortal, you get along with everyone, you understand me and why I didn't tell you sooner, and you're very trustable.

"I am only like the man you love because I'm immortal. If I wasn't immortal and was born at this time, I guarantee you that you wouldn't like me. No one would. I would just be an average loser." He laid back down, taking me with him.

"Felix… No…"

I began, trying to find the right words, but his expression after I began talking said it all, he read my mind, he saw the positive words I thought about him, he saw the sad images I pictured of him if he wasn't immortal.

His gaze became loving, and he smiled. "You really think that about me?" I nodded, making *him* blush for the second time *ever.* (At least he claims he's never blushed before he found me)

"God, I love you. How did I get *so* lucky in all of your lifetimes?" He kissed me, eventually moving his lips to my cheeks and my jaw.

"What do you mean; 'all of my lifetimes'?" I asked after he got down to my neck, worrying I ruined the moment with my curiosity.

"Ever since I first met you in 1873, one hundred and fifty years ago, you weren't Carmen obviously. You were a woman named Caroline.

Caroline West. You were a very spoiled girl, yet you were abused by your father. I only ended up meeting you because my 'mother' at that time was going to check in on *your* mother, who was dying of some disease. That was the first time I saw you, but definitely not the last.

"I asked your father's permission to take you on a date, and since I was rich, he agreed. I brought you on a lovely date. We went to a movie theater, a rose field like the one we are in now, and on a boat ride across the rivers in Paris. And then my mother made you her maid, causing me to fall in love with you even more as I saw you everyday. You died a little bit after I told you that I loved you.

"Before you died and before you were my mother's maid, we saw each other in an art gallery and we had run into each other a couple of times prior. I walked up to you, looking at the painting of a red rose you stood at for so long. I asked if you liked roses and you were startled, yet replied with, 'I say yes, they have a meaning that triggers some memories I don't quite remember.'" He smiled as I quietly repeated the words at the same time as him.

"Carmen... I have a surprise for you." He smiled, closing his eyes as I saw a veil of golden light flash before my eyes. We suddenly weren't in the flower field anymore. We were in a spectacular pavilion with the sunset in the distance.

"This is a special pavilion I created for you. We can go back and watch or *relive* memories from our past whenever we want. I thought you'd like to go back and experience some of these memories I love so dearly."

"*Relive?* We can *relive* the past?" He nodded, "Can we right now?" My eyes grew impatient.

"Yes," He chuckled, "Close your eyes."

Thirteen

"Caroline!" A male voice yelled, I turned to face the man "Hello Caroline." He smiled a wide, toothy smile.

'It's Sir Felix!' I thought, recognizing him at once.

"Enjoying that rose painting I see?" He chuckled.

"I say yes, they have a meaning that triggers some memories I don't quite remember." I scratched my head, rubbing the itchy hair clip I wore.

"Ah, I see." He picked my hand up, "May I?" He asked politely.

I nodded and he pushed my hand to his lips, setting a soft kiss on my pale hand. I blushed a bright pink, wishing that the act of hello could have been something more. He smiled as if he heard my thoughts.

"Do you like roses, Sir Felix?"

"Please, just call me Felix." He chuckled, "Yes, I do. They mean a lot to me." He smiled brighter.

"How so?" I asked, and his eyebrows furrowed, "I'm sorry, you don't have to explain…"

"No, it's alright. I see them as a symbol of love. If you can't tell someone you love them, show them, by giving them something that symbols your love." He handed me a bouquet of roses, chuckling as blood flushed to my cheeks.

"I-" I began, being cut off when his hand went to my blonde, wavy hair, and him pulling me closer by my waist.

"Caroline. I love you." I blushed brighter which I didn't think was possible. He put his forehead on mine, "May I?" He asked again and I nodded.

He pressed his soft pink lips to mine, his hand trailing down my hair and to my neck and eventually my jaw, holding my head still. People in the gallery looked at us but Felix didn't mind. People were whispering, asking why *Sir Felix* was kissing *me*, a spoiled girl who had nothing to offer.

"Felix…" I moaned softly, being cut off by another passionate kiss.

"Caroline… Will you do me the wonderful honor?" He paused, knowing I knew what he was asking.

"Yes! Yes yes!" I yelled and kissed him. I pulled away, clearing my throat and mouthing the words 'I apologize' to the people around us who were gaping at the scene. He laughed and smiled, pulling me into another kiss.

There was a sudden tug at my arm, causing me to get out of the scene. "Carmen~" Felix sang, alerting my ears and causing my eyes to flash open. "Did you enjoy that?" He laughed, "I've been trying to get your attention for the past three minutes." I blushed, laying my head down on his lap.

Felix moved us from the pavilion to the flower field. We were sitting, my head still in his lap as he smoothed out my hair, causing me to flinch

"Energy still super noticeable?" He asked, taking his hand away from my hair and placing it down on my upper thigh. I nodded and he set a small kiss on my forehead. "Sorry, love."

I closed my eyes, wishing I could go to sleep. He noticed and flashed us over to the house, carrying me bridal style to our room, and setting me on the bed.

"You can't sleep, but you *can* relax and close your eyes. It gives your brain time to rest. I don't personally do it, but Carly and Alice do. They say it's 'refreshing'."

"Okay," I choked out, the thirst coming back. Felix noticed, manifesting that infinite bottle back in my hand.

"Drink as much as you need. I don't judge."

After he said that I chugged as much of the red liquid as I could, not having to pause for a breath. I drank about another gallon full and I finally set it on the bedside table.

"Better?" Felix smiled. His face was patient and relaxed as I nodded. He climbed into bed with me, wrapping his arms around me like he always does and pulling me closer to his chest. "I miss doing this." He kissed the top of my head as my eyes shut.

My mind relaxed, playing back the scene in the theater, imagining myself as Caroline again, kissing Felix as if my life depended on it. Suddenly, there was a knock at the front door, followed by a doorbell ring.

"Oh shit…" Felix stood up, releasing me from his grasp. He walked to the closed bedroom door and held it open. "C'mon," He gestured his head to the door, making me stand up and go through it.

When we went downstairs Francis, Alice, Carly, Josh, and Seth were there, all dressed in sleek black outfits.

"Get her changed. We have got to get ready." Francis said as Felix allowed them in. Felix nodded, bringing me upstairs quickly.

"Throw those on." He motioned to the bed, looking at the black leather jacket, black tank top, and black jeans. "Please, love." He added, noticing I was confused and worried.

"Are we starting a rock band or something?" I joked, earning nothing more but a deep nose exhale from him. I noticed now wasn't the time to joke and got ready.

"Could you explain what exactly is happening?" I asked, looking over at Felix who was fully dressed in black dress pants and a black long-sleeve button-up.

"Yeah, It's almost midnight. Floyd and his group are on the way. They are willing to listen for a *little*, but that's it. We just thought it'd be nice to be organized and look put together." He folded the cuffs of his shirt, exhaling hard through his nose. I looked over at the clock '11:34' it read, causing me to panic.

"What if they decide to not hear us through, or… Or maybe… What if they-" I stuttered, being cut off by a deep, thought-clearing kiss, causing me to relax a little bit.

"It's alright~" Felix cooed, pulling me tightly to his chest, one of his arms around my waist, the other set softly on the back of my head.

"I think I'm ready." I lifted my head out of the crook of his neck, looking up at him. Tears stung in my eyes and I blinked, letting them out by accident.

"Oh, baby…" Felix pulled me back into his warm grasp, "Let's just relax for a little bit." He smoothed out my hair, kissing my cheek, trying to calm me down.

"I'm alright-" I started, my voice hoarse and scratchy.

"No," Was all he replied with, knowing I knew what he meant. We were in each other's embrace until the clock read *'11:39'*. Felix finally disconnected with a small kiss on the top of my head. At that kiss a weird wave of energy went through me, making me not like the fact he had just kissed me multiple times.

"We've got to go get ready." He noticed the confusion on my face, "Training. We gotta tell you how to do certain things just in case." I followed him downstairs, being met with everyone just relaxing in the foyer.

"We've gotta hurry," Francis grabbed Alice's arm and tugged her outside, all of us following.

Felix and I got into his car. Felix manifested the elixir back, setting it in the cupholder. "Just in case," He smiled, that smile turning into a frown as he saw my worried expression. "It'll be okay. I *promise.*" I nodded, looking out the window. I wanted to scream as I suddenly had no want to talk or be around him. What was happening?

"Carmen... Please speak, love. It hurts to not hear your voice." He reached for my hand but I pulled away, setting it down on my lap. "Did I do something? Please tell me, baby." I didn't reply.

I don't know why I was acting like this, it was as if something was affecting my brain, causing me to not be so fond of Felix at the moment. He tried looking through my thoughts, giving up after figuring out that the amount of the elixir I drank affected my thoughts and how easy they were to read.

"Carmen..." He reached a hand up to my face, and turned my head to face him, making me close my eyes. "What did I do? What's wrong?" I just exhaled hard. What was *wrong* with me? I was ignoring my smart, patient, caring, and sexy boyfriend, for no reason at all.

'It's not you. I don't know what's wrong, I'm not mad at you, I **swear**.*"* I tried sending a telepathic message but he shook his head, manifesting a red rose and setting it on the dashboard as if he didn't get my message.

'Carmen, I'm not sure what I did. Please forgive me, love. I can't look into your thoughts, or see any messages, but please just know I love you and that I would never intentionally hurt you. Please give me some sort of sign if you understand.' He started the car, hoping, praying even, for me to send some type of sign to know that I wasn't mad.

All I did was exhale hard again, turning my head back and out of his strong grasp. He exhaled too, pulling the car out of the drive and following the others.

We sat in silence for the rest of the ride, Felix sending me messages every now and then, and me taking them in, yet not being able to respond, send a sign, *nothing*. I was heartbroken to see Felix like this, his not understanding that I wasn't in control of my own body was terrible. I turned my head a bit, grabbing the elixir out of the cup holder as it suddenly disappeared.

"Tell me what I did wrong. *Please.*" I looked up at Felix, my amazing, smart, caring, and hot boyfriend, who was now getting upset with *me*. The *monster* inside of me is taking *over*.

"Don't look at me. Don't talk to me. I've had enough with you." My voice said sharply, my face reflecting the opposite. I tried shaking my head but Felix handed me the bottle.

"Alright…" He turned his head back to the road, lots of thoughts flowing through his head. *'Is she okay?'*, *'I have to tell Francis. We can't go into this fight with her not trusting me.'* and, *'Carmen, love. Please wake up. I know you don't hate me.'* being the loudest ones I heard.

'Francis. I don't know what's wrong but my body and mind are mad at Felix. Please tell him I'm not mad and that I care about him. He's hurt, but my mind won't give in. Won't apologize. I don't know what is happening.' If this didn't work, I wasn't sure what I was going to do.

Felix, my *forever* partner—my *soulmate*—was hurt by me, my actions, and my words. Yet, those things weren't me. There was something wrong with me. His eyes grew worried, yet relaxed.

'*I got Francis's message about you. I don't know what's happening either. If I had to guess I'd assume it was Freya, Floyd, or his minions. They control the mind and body, they could be causing you to do this.*' He turned to look over at me, calming his breathing as my body turned to face the window again.

"Carmen, love. *Try*. Try to talk, try to move your hand to mine. *Anything*. Please, darling." My eyes just closed, my face tightening. He gave up after that.

When we got back to Francis and Alice's house I dashed out of the car and ran away from Felix. He flashed over to us as well.

"I know you don't mean it, it's okay."

"What's wrong with her?" Carly asked, walking up to Felix and putting her arm around his shoulders.

"She- uh…" He tried getting an explanation out but shook his head, "I have a feeling Floyd or Freya have something to do with this."

"It's 11:54," Francis announced and we all nodded. "Carmen come with me, please." He walked to his car and took out an orange drink from a plastic water bottle.

"What *is* that?"

"Medicine. Drink it, please." I nodded and drank it, my eyes closed and when I opened them everything was vibrant again.

"There, your mind is blocked. Freya was controlling your thoughts about Felix." I blinked a lot, trying to calm the vibrant colors down.

"So I'm not mad at him anymore?" He shook his head.

"You shouldn't be." He smiled, gesturing back to the group. I ran up to Felix, latching myself around his waist and laying my head in the crook of his neck, sending little kisses over his jaw, ear, and neck.

"I'm so sorry, Felix. I don't know what happened. I'm so so sorry." His arms wrapped around my waist.

"It's okay, love. It's okay~" He cooed, kissing me as I kissed him.

"Shit... We've gotta go, they're almost here." Felix set me down on the ground and held my hand, speeding us over to the river with everyone else.

Fourteen

Floyd, Esther, and Freya, plus some new faces were standing over across the river, looking over at us. There were about 100 other immortals standing behind them dressed in red cloaks, with the exception of Floyd, Esther, Freya, and two other guys dressed in black cloaks with red fabric on the inside of the large hoods.

"Carmen, I'm so glad we could finally meet." Floyd cleared his throat, his deep voice revealed the soft voice he truly had. He cleared his throat again, hinting to the group of people behind him to take a big step back. I swallowed hard, worrying that he was already ready to fight. "I see that you're immortal now… How interesting."

"It was an accident!" Felix butted in, covering his mouth after he said it.

"Defensive I see." Floyd chuckled, cocking his head a tiny bit.

"I'm sorry…" Felix whispered to me.

"And I *also* see that you figured out the little joke we played on you. I'm glad that you figured out how to finish it." He smiled a fake smile., "Freya, apologize for that cruel joke Esther and you played." He looked over at Freya, her face blank.

"I'm so truly sorry, Carmen." Her mouth curved up a little bit. Freya stepped forward, Esther and the two others following.

"Did I not introduce them?" Floyd asked, seeing my expression in reaction to the other two guys that were in red cloaks. "This is Lawrence and Reuben. They are my sons." He looked at the people behind him. "Let's not dilly-dally, hey? Let's get on with it." Everyone in red cloaks flashed over the river, making us step back.

"How exactly was this an *accident*, Felix?" Floyd stepped toward Felix. I tried to walk backward with him but he rubbed my hand and then stayed there, standing right in front of Floyd. *'Be careful, I'll be okay.'* Felix sent and I nodded.

"I swear this was an accident. We had a party at our house and I thought we put the elixir away but we didn't put it away *well enough.*"

"Would you mind if Freya could look at this memory?" Floyd turned his gaze to me, cocking his head. I nodded and stepped forward. "Freya, come." Freya stepped forward as well, her and I being right next to each other as she pressed her cold hand to my chest, causing me to gasp like the first time.

She held her hand there for a while. "I can't get a good read. Floyd you may want to see for yourself." She removed her hand and stepped back letting Floyd see for himself.

Floyd put his hand out in front of him, gesturing for me to put my hand in his. I looked back to Felix and he nodded. I placed my hand in Floyd's strong, warm grasp. He pulled me closer to him, making the air in my throat come out in a loud gasp.

"It wasn't an accident." Floyd lied, opening his eyes and looking at me. "They're telling a lie."

Felix's eyes went wide, causing my senses to go off the rails.

"We aren't lying!" Carly butted in, causing Freya to paralyze her. Carly fell to the floor and her eyes fluttered shut. Josh and Seth ran up to her, looking up at Freya. She stopped as Esther patted her shoulder,

"If you say you're not lying... I guess a fight might be the only way to solve this." Floyd peered at Francis and Alice.

"There will be no fighting, Floyd." Francis stepped forward, placing a hand on my shoulder, taking it off almost immediately after knowing that energy currents were really strong right now.

"Why, dear *brother*?" Floyd took a step forward as well. Felix and I stepped back from them.

'Brother? Why wouldn't he have told us this?' I thought. Felix looked down at me and squeezed my hand.

'He didn't want to scare you. Technically they aren't biological brothers, but back when Francis became immortal, he wasn't the only one. He saved a lot of people, thinking immortality was the solution to the small problem.' Felix didn't

finish what he said, he was distracted from the situation going on.

"Floyd. Let's not do this now." Francis backed away, resulting in Floyd taking a step forward again.

"Why not, Francis?" He smiled, "We haven't fought since we parted ways oh so long ago."

"Floyd…" Francis started, being cut off by Floyd and his story.

"Ever since 1319, we have been enemies. I figured out how to make an immortal elixir and that made you hate me. I'm not so sure why you gave the elixir of life to all of those people if you were just going to leave. So I made an elixir like yours, just using more blood. Blood from all the immortals that killed themselves knowing that they would be seen as a threat and be killed anyways.

"You left us all to die, keeping that special elixir for yourself. You ran away to France, wanting to start fresh. You made that choice. Kind of like how everyone behind me made the choice to follow *me*. The person that made an elixir, moved them away from the immortals' execution, and cared for them." He paused, gesturing his arms around his side like wings to show the immortals behind him.

"I actually cared for them. I knew what you did was bad, but I couldn't risk all these important immortals to just be killed or kill themselves out of guilt. We live happily, and I see that you do too, with your own little immortal family. Including the **newborn** *Carmen*." He spoke my name like it was a curse. I hated the way it rolled off his tongue with little effort.

"Which I'm sure you haven't even told Carmen about our *exchanges* in the past, hmm?" He smiled again, looking over at me and Felix, looking down at our hands that were interlocked tightly. "I can see you haven't." He looked back at Francis, referring to the fact that our hands were interlocked so tight due to the new information I had just received.

"What does this have to do with Carmen?" Francis asked impatiently.

"I just thought it'd be nice to remind you, brother. And to tell the newborn. But I suppose you're going to whine over the fact that it was an accident and that there was *'no harm done'* as I believe you used to phrase it." He cleared his throat as his British accent came out strong as he said that.

"She isn't a threat. She is an *immortal*." Francis flashed his amber eyes over to Freya's red ones, glaring at her for only a second.

"How can we be so sure?" A deep, British voice came from Lawrence. His voice was thirsty, husky, and impatient.

"Now now, Lawrence." Floyd looked back at him, "She isn't a human. Her blood won't be appealing." He smiled a wide grin. "I *would* find it appealing to fight, though." He looked at Francis again, his bright red eyes practically glowing.

"No. No fighting." Francis insisted, looking at Alice.

"We might have to if they don't believe us, Francis," Alice whispered.

"I won't risk anyone's life." His eyes turned back to Floyd.

"Well... I guess we have no choice." He smiled brighter, "Immortals? Fi-"

"Wait!" Felix interjected, "This will not work."

"What- How could you be *sure?*" Floyd stepped over to Felix as he let go of my hand making me want to jump forward and push Floyd's head into the ground.

"I can see it. I can read thoughts, along with seeing big events in the future. If we fight, you will die, so will we." Felix swallowed hard, looking at me quickly.

"Let me see," Floyd demanded, grabbing Felix's hand in his own. He closed his eyes, taking in the new information of what will happen.

"The boy is right. If we fight, we will die. Not all of us, but most of us. Carmen and Felix would run away, leaving their family to defend themselves. If we fight, nothing will be resolved, it will just make things worse. But does that prove why *not* fight? No. Not really.

"What do we say, immortals? Do we save a fight for today, leaving dirt to clean in the future? Or do we fight now? Killing off most of us? The choice is up to the majority of the votes." He turned around, looking at the sea of red cloaks. "Raise your hand and speak up if you think we *should* fight today."

He smiled wider causing me to cringe back worried. About fifteen of the one-hundred immortals raised their hands, chanting "Fight," over and over again.

"I see no fighting wins. What a shame." He turned back to us, "I suppose I should explain your consequences for bringing another immortal into the world, Francis." He called Freya ahead and both she and Esther walked forward, standing on opposite sides of him, still about three yards away from us.

"Freya, why don't you show them what Esther taught you?" Freya nodded, looking over at me and Felix. Her face relaxed, scaring me. "Hate," Was all she said, causing me to snag my hand away from Felix's.

"Love, don't fall for it." He whispered right before I flashed over to Carly instead. "Francis…" He looked at Francis, seeing him nod.

A bottle of orange liquid in a water bottle appeared in his hand. He handed it to me, smiling. I took it and swigged it down, the monster inside of me disappearing. I flashed over back to Felix and held his hand again.

"Sorry…" I whispered, feeling ashamed.

"It's alright, Carmen." He looked at Freya again, "Do you need any more evidence or are we just going to fight?" He swallowed hard, his other hand wrapped tightly into a ball.

"I'll follow what the other immortals say. Although, Felix, your *father* may have to pay the price. We could either reverse his immortality or we could kill him, or maybe we could just make him join our side." He smiled, glaring at Francis ever so slightly.

"I will not join your side. And I will *not* be reversing my immortality." Francis stepped forward, not ahead of Felix and me.

"And you won't kill him, either!" Alice blurted, her face terrified.

"Ah, *Alice*." Floyd started, "My sister-in-law. How are you? Good? That's good." He asked although he couldn't care less, "What do *you* suggest we do to him? We *have* to do something." He smiled again, glaring at *her* now.

"What if we swear to never make someone immortal again, this was an accident and could have been avoided if we only hid the drink better." She stopped looking over at me.

'It could have been avoided if I wasn't so stupid...' I thought, causing Felix to look down at me and squeeze my hand tighter.

"Don't think of yourself like that. It's not your fault, it's okay.' He sent me, trying to calm me down but only making it worse. He rubbed his thumb over my hand, helping a little bit with the calm tone.

Floyd didn't talk for a while, possibly thinking of an answer, listening to Felix and I's 'private' conversation, or just stalling to make time.

"Hmm... We'd have to think that one out. I'm not sure if we can trust you guys." He cocked his head, 'pondering' the situation. "I suppose we could give it a try. But if you break that promise, we'll be back… Trust me, dear family." He turned around, putting his hands forward like a conductor, and as soon as they all came, they were gone. All except for one little girl.

"Can we help you?" Alice asked, walking up to the little girl. She reached her hand out to touch the girl but she ran away into the forest, following the others.

Carly flashed back to the house, we followed to see what was wrong. "Leave me alone!" She screamed, causing us to step back and watch as she ran to her room.

"Carly, what's wrong?" Francis asked calmly, following Carly up the stairs and leaning against her door as she slammed it in his face.

"She paralyzed me! What *isn't* wrong?" She yelled through the door and started sobbing. I took off my leather jacket and handed it to Felix. I flashed up the stairs to Francis and nodded at him, telling him to let me handle it.

"Carly? May I come in?" I knew she was leaning up against the door, her knees held up to her chest as she sobbed into her pants. Although, I'm not sure *how* I knew that.

*'Only if it's **just you'*** She sent me, and I nodded even though she couldn't see it. She went away from her door and cracked it open slightly, allowing me in. I walked in cautiously and sat on the floor right in front of the door.

"You wanna talk about it?" I offered, looking at her with the calmest, most caring face I could make.

"Oliver was in the group of immortals standing behind Floyd..." She raised her voice slightly and looked up at me, then set her head back in her hands.

"I..." I tried to talk but my voice wouldn't allow it. How could he do that to her? After they had been together for centuries. "Maybe he had a good-" She cut me off.

"His eyes were bright red. He drank their elixir. He had an option, they don't just give their magical potion out to anyone. But *you* wouldn't know that." She looked up at me through her eyebrows, anger in her now deep red eyes.

"D-Do you think *I* did this? Carly, I had *nothing* to do with this!" I protested, causing her to stand up.

"If you didn't *fucking* drink the elixir we wouldn't have been in this mess! Hell, if you hadn't gotten together with the '*hot, smart, know-it-all*', this wouldn't have happened *at all*!" She yelled, mocking my voice poorly.

"This is *not my fault*." I stood up as well, my hand clutched at my side.

She looked down at my fist and then back up at me, her eyes now a bright red. "*I hate you,*

Carmen!" She yelled as I heard Felix flash up the stairs.

"What makes you think *I* caused this?" I yelled back, matching her energy.

"Oliver told me he felt guilty for what happened to you. He said he should've hidden the elixir better." She closed her eyes for a second, opening them again when Felix rushed in.

"What is happening?" Felix looked at Carly and her red eyes, "Carmen, get out." He turned to face me, his eyes scared. "Now." He demanded and I nodded.

He closed the door behind me and I heard a smack of some sort. Felix walked back out after a little bit.

"What happened? Where is she?"

"I took care of her."

Fifteen

"What do you mean you 'took care of her'?" I stopped Felix before he could walk down the stairs.

"I took care of her." He shrugged, looking down at our interlocked hands.

"No. Tell me what you *mean*." I demanded.

"I knocked her out." His face showed no emotion.

"What the hell, Felix?" I furrowed my eyebrows, pulling my hand away.

"Love, you don't understand-"

"Oh so it's another *'you wouldn't understand because you're a newer immortal'*, huh?" I spat out, cutting him off and looking at him with disgust and confusion.

"*Carmen...*" He furrowed his eyebrows slightly, his tone raising a bit.

"No no no, you have *no* right to be upset with *me*. *You're* the one who won't explain a damn thing!" I clicked my tongue and looked at the wall. "What did she *do?*" I pursed my lips together, refusing to look at him until he gave an explanation.

"Darling... Can we *please* talk about this later?" He folded his arms against his chest, leaning against the wall slightly. I shook my head and looked at him. I rolled my eyes as I sucked my teeth, showing my anger and disapproval of his answer. "Fine, let's talk about it now then."

"What did you *do*?" I asked again, this time not accepting 'you don't understand' as an answer.

"Something was wrong with her. You saw her red eyes, didn't you?" I nodded and he continued, "She was about to attack me so I hit her weakest point, knocking her out."

"I thought immortals couldn't get hurt?" I cocked my head slightly.

"Yes and no. All immortals have a weak point. Her weak point is at the tip of her nose, one harsh touch and she'll be out."

"Do you know *why* she was like that?"

"No, not exactly. I know she was angry because of the Floyd and Oliver situation, I just can't explain why her eyes were red. All I know is that it has something to do with Floyd."

"What do you think Floyd has to do with it?"

"Didn't she tell you; '*His eyes were red, he drank the elixir.*'?" I nodded, "One sip of their elixir can make you so thirsty for human blood your eyes turn red. I have a feeling she drank their elixir somehow."

"How? We were with her the entire time."

"I don't know, love." He exhaled softly.

"Then why are you assuming?-" I began, being cut off by Felix.

"There isn't another explanation I can think of right now. Can we *please* just talk about this later?" He looked at me with impatient eyes. Something was off.

"What's wrong?" I held his hand in mine, looking back at him softly.

"Nothing," He tried to convince me but I shook my head, completely ignoring the fact we just fought. "Really, it's nothing." He smiled, bringing my hand to his lips, and placing a soft kiss on my pale skin.

"Alright," I looked down at our hands, my head suddenly going dizzy.

"Carmen? Carmen?" Felix's voice seemed distant, underwater, almost. "Carmen!" He yelled as I fell, his voice only ringing in my ears as a low hum.

When I awoke I was resting on Felix's chest as he smoothed out my hair.

"You alright, love?" He moved his hand to my back, noticing I was awake. I nodded, my voice not wanting to form words. "You fainted. I'm just assuming it's because it's been a while since you drank the elixir."

"Maybe..." My voice was faint and squeaky, "What time is it?" I tried to look up at the clock but he set me back down on his chest softly.

"4:17 at night. It's been a while since you passed out."

"I thought immortals couldn't-" I began, being cut off by Felix.

"We thought so, too. Francis is going to test you after you're better."

"I'm better now-" I tried to protest but Felix shook his head.

"No. You're *not*." He said, almost instantly manifesting a rose for me and setting it on the bedside table. I exhaled hard and tried to show my disapproval but he just chuckled, placing a kiss on the top of my head.

Some time passed and after a while Francis walked in, "I'd like to do the tests now if that's alright." He smiled a warm smile, trying to showcase that everything was okay. I nodded and sat up, Felix followed my actions shortly after.

"I'd like to do a heart scan of both of you, just to see and show the difference between you and Felix, if that's alright with you." I took Felix's hand and nodded. "Could you please sit on that table right there?" He asked as he gestured us into his workroom.

The room he worked in was full of medical equipment that glew a bright yellow, illuminating the room. There was a black medical table in the middle of the room, a white knit blanket draped over it neatly.

"You can change the colors if you'd prefer a different color." He nodded his head at the small little black remote on the table. The table held a vase of sunflowers and a family photo he kept.

"That's better," I grabbed the remote, changed the color to purple, and smiled, looking up at Felix.

"Lay on the bed, please." Francis motioned to the black sleek bed in the middle of the room. I sat on the bed and Francis moved over a device that hovered over my head and chest.

"Can I watch something?" I asked as I noticed the little TV screen above my head in the contraption. He nodded and handed me a remote. I pressed the '2' button and it switched to *Spongebob Squarepants*, and I decided to just relax and watch it.

Francis walked over to his desk and I heard the machine switch on as a little whirring went through the air. There was a slight vibration from the machine, making me jump in response.

"It's okay, there's nothing to worry about." Felix rubbed my hand with his thumb, trying to comfort me even though I *wasn't* scared.

"I know," I whispered as I flinched again when another vibration went through the machine, still keeping my eyes forward so as to not disturb the scans.

After about ten minutes of sitting there, Francis turned the machine off, and the TV paused, eventually fading out soon after.

"This is strange," Francis admitted, moving the machine away. "It looks as if your body is trying to keep your heart pumping. Refusing to let go." He rubbed his chin, his slight stubble making a small scratching sound.

I looked at the monitor sitting in front of me and noticed the picture of my heart. *I* couldn't tell what was wrong, but the way Felix and Francis were reacting, something was *wrong*. Francis looked at me, his eyes furrowed.

"This is why I wish we had a human scan right now." He said, walking back over to his computer. "Give me one second."

"What exactly is wrong?" I whispered to Felix, my hand still in his.

"Your heart is…" He paused, hesitating to tell me. "Well, it's getting smaller, more shriveled. We're thinking it's because of how much elixir you're drinking, but it wouldn't explain why it's still beating." He exhaled hard.

"Felix, no. It's *not* your fault." His eyes opened a little more, probably because he isn't used to me reading his mind or being able to *sense* when he is feeling down.

"I-" He began, closing his mouth after he realized he had nothing to say. Francis came over shortly after, explaining to us the difference between my scans and the human scan.

"See how your heart scan is smaller than this scan?" He pointed to the human scan, "I took one of the scans you've had before this and that's what we're comparing." He cleared his throat and then switched the images to Felix's heart scans versus the human scans. "This is what Felix's heart looks like. Even after almost 300 years, it looks relatively similar to the human heart, just not pumping as much blood." He clicked his tongue and kept his face calm.

"Could we inject blood into my heart?" It was a dumb question that slipped out, causing me not to act surprised because of my words.

"The problem is that your heart *won't stop* beating." He shook his head, "If we injected more blood, your heart would take it in and continue beating. I'm not sure what we *can* do in this situation. As an immortal, I've never had this happen in my 700 years." He furrowed his eyebrow, looking back at my scans.

"And she just *has* to be the first?" Felix asked, scared for me.

"Unfortunately," He looked to Felix, "Maybe fate has something to do with this. Maybe this is happening because she *shouldn't* be immortal." He paused, looking at me, "Maybe not." He added, turning off the monitor.

"Are we free to go?" I asked and he nodded.

"Yes, go ahead. I just ask that we do this again before you two leave. I want to know you're safe before you go hours away." I nodded and Felix took my hand, pulling me out of that room.

"I- What's happening to me?" I asked, my breath trembling.

"I'm not sure, love." He looked down at our hands, still pulling me out of their house and to our house for the next couple of days.

When we arrived at the house he walked me to the kitchen, saying he was going to *'try something'*.

"You hungry? Tired? Anything *human*?" He asked, looking in the fridge.

"Not really- Felix, what are you doing?" I moved onto one of the tan bar stools we had on our island and grabbed his hand over the counter when he turned to face me. "What's wrong?" I asked, my face calm and collected, my mind worried and confused.

"It's nothing, darling. I swear. I just want to test something." I didn't protest anymore but he knew I didn't believe him.

He grabbed a container of yogurt out of the fridge, putting some into a wooden bowl that was in the cabinet.

"Baby… what're you doing?"

"Shh~" He leaned over the island and put a finger to my lips. He started putting fruit into the bowl and made it look nice before putting a golden spoon in it and spinning it toward me.

"Try this, please." He smiled when I picked up the spoon and brought it to my mouth. "What does it *taste* like?" He put his elbows on the counter and his head in his hands, looking at me with desperate, loving eyes.

"It tastes like yogurt…" I smiled at the sight, still confused, though.

"Alright," He kept his bright white smile on his face.

"What is it *supposed* to taste like?" I wasn't sure if it was *supposed* to taste like yogurt or not.

"For certain immortals, it tastes like nothing. For *others,* it tastes like yogurt." He moved his hands to be in front of himself.

"So… I'm not immortal?…" I put my hands on top of his, my voice calm yet confused.

"You're immortal, I promise you that." He chuckled lightly, still smiling and looking at me with his pretty, loving, caring, and patient eyes.

"So why did it taste like yogurt?" I asked, manifesting a rose for him.

"I'm not sure, I just wanted to try something."

He took my hand and walked me to our room, pushing me back on the bed and hovering himself over me.

"I hate fighting with you, love. I really do. I'm sorry," He apologized as he kissed my neck, making me forget the fight and succeeding in sending a shiver down my spine.

"Me too," I smiled and looked at him, I mean *really* looked at him for the first time as an immortal. His beautiful, bright, hazel eyes, messy blond hair, and sparkling white teeth.

My eyes traveled all throughout him, looking at the band t-shirt he wore, his dark gray slacks, the bracelet he had on that I had made for him at a camp I went to last year, and the orange amulet he wore around his neck. I reached my hand up to touch it but he grabbed my wrist and shook his head, telling me not to.

"Love, no." He still kept that warm smile on his face, holding my wrist tightly in his hand.

"Sorry..." He let go of my wrist and shifted himself a little bit.

"It's alright, it didn't hurt." I reminded him, smiling back.

We sat like that for a while but eventually, he convinced me to look at myself in the mirror, as I haven't since I was a human. "C'mon, you're so pretty and you haven't even *looked*!" He sat me up and walked over to the mirror, holding out a hand for me to grab.

"Fine~" I whined, following him with a smile on my face.

I walked up to the large gold mirror and peered at him before I moved in front of it to see myself. He had opened the curtains so the light shone and made the experience even more memorable. I looked at his messy hair which is a mix of golden yellow and light brown. I looked at his golden, hazel eyes and his light pink, plump lips. His slightly tan skin practically glowed due to the open curtains.

I looked at the mirror itself, the golden rim being reflective due to the light. The heart-shaped on the top of the mirror was a diamond that sparkled in the light, the light from the diamond bouncing off on Felix.

I looked at the ground, at my feet, my red-painted toenails that Felix must have manifested. I took a step forward and moved my head up slowly. I stopped when my eyes reached my legs, no longer a trace of hair on my pale, exposed calves, no more bruises on my thighs, none of it.

I stopped my eyes again when they reached my torso. My white tank top was pulled up a little bit, exposing my belly button and where my surgery scars used to be. All gone. I looked at my arms, no trace of the burn scars I had on my left arm from when I was cooking as a kid. Luckily, my skin was still relatively the same, my freckles and moles still being there.

I moved my eyes up a little more and looked at the lower half of my face. My neck was more prominent, my lips darker and plumper, and my pimples were gone along with my black-heads.

I moved my gaze to meet my eyes, looking at my full reflection, and not seeing *me*. Seeing the girl I'd always *dreamed* of looking like. No blemishes, no bruises, no scars, nothing.

My 'sky blue' eyes were really that, sky blue as Felix had described them. I noticed the slight pink tint I had over my cheeks, making me flush more. I looked at my hair, my natural, light blonde hair, my '*Elsa* hair' as some little kids had called it before.

"Beautiful," Felix snaked an arm around my waist and looked down at the real me as I looked at him in the mirror. "*Do* you see just *how* beautiful you are, darling? If you don't think you look amazing then I don't think we're looking at the same person, then." He smiled, placing kisses on my cheek.

"I-" I began, pausing as I was at a loss for words. "I look great…" I said, although, I didn't sound happy.

"You don't like what you see." It wasn't a question but a statement. "Are you not happy with how you look?" He asked, pulling his lips away from my cheek.

"Of course, I'm happy, I look like the goddess I've always *wanted* to be. But I guess after a lifetime of looking like how I did… This is… Strange." I admitted, my voice soft and quiet, not wanting to sound greedy.

"I understand that. I'd be quite shocked if I saw the world as a human again for the first time in 300 years." He chuckled softly, trying to lighten the mood.

All I did was stand there, taking in my body, my face, my new *form*. I looked so different… and I wasn't sure how I felt about it. His arm tightened around my waist and he brought a hand up to my chin, making me face him.

"Love, you're gorgeous… okay? I understand you aren't used to it, but not liking it isn't going to make it go away. You need to *accept* it." He kissed my nose, letting go of my waist and walking back over to the bed.

After we got situated in bed he told me that I should try to rest my mind again since I didn't get too much before. I agreed— although I didn't want to—and set my head on his chest, closing my eyes and relaxing as he hummed my song

"I love you," He told me right before I lost consciousness.

Sixteen

My dream was peaceful and quiet, yet scary. Scary because I wasn't expecting it. Immortals *aren't* supposed to dream, yet I did.

Immortals *aren't* supposed to pass out, yet I did. Immortals' hearts aren't supposed to be beating so much, yet mine *is*. Something is wrong, we all knew *that*.

"Why are you being so distant?" A faint female voice echoed, "Why don't you talk to us anymore?" It continued.

"We're your friends, why don't you seem to care about us anymore?" A voice I instantly recognized as Alex asked, making me assume the other voices were Jenny and Harley.

"Where did you go? You ran off with Felix and we haven't seen you since." Harley's voice sounded sad, making me feel bad about being so distant from my friends. My amazing, caring, thoughtful friends who would never leave me as I left them.

"You didn't even say *goodbye*." Jenny's voice explained as the dark void of my mind was changed to the pavilion that Felix had manifested for me. He sat by my side as he looked at the screen in front of us.

"Do you ever regret your past?" He asked, his eyes still dead ahead.

"I mean... Yeah... Why?" I asked, looking at him with furrowed eyebrows.

"I always wonder what would've happened if I didn't meet you. This whole *thing* wouldn't have been so *terrible*. I could have still been in France for all I know." He closed his eyes slowly, opening them again when I spoke.

"Felix," I began, my voice cracked due to the sudden surprise in what he said. "D-Did I do something?" My voice pitched higher than normal as tears slowly stung my eyes.

"I was just thinking. Maybe I *shouldn't* have saved you. Maybe you were better off without me. Maybe *I* was better off without *you*." He shifted himself to move away from me a little.

"Felix…" My voice cracked again, causing me to stop talking and look down at my fingers.

"I shouldn't have saved you. You think every little inconvenience is your fault, even if it has *nothing* to do with you." He scoffed, standing up. "You can figure out how to manifest *yourself at home*." He spat, vanishing out of the pavilion shortly after.

I brought a hand up to my mouth and let the tears fall from my eyes. How could he say *that*? I really thought he loved me. I guess I was just dumb after all.

I tried a couple of times to manifest myself in a flower field but settled when I managed to teleport myself to the room we'd been sleeping in for the past week, landing on the bed, laying alone. I got up off the bed and grabbed a bag from the closet. I heard shuffling happening downstairs but didn't pay attention to it as I packed some clothes, a blanket, a pillow, books, makeup, and hygiene products into my messenger bag. I sensed Felix walk in shortly after, he had something in his hand, but I didn't even care to figure out what.

"I know you want me gone. I'll be leaving in a second." I announced, not caring to meet his gaze.

"What?" He paused, taking in what I had said. "Love, I don't want you gone. What're you talking about?"

He set the wooden tray of breakfast food and the bouquet of flowers on the white cushion bench at the foot of the bed. He walked up to me but I just faced the opposite way, looking at the wall, trying not to cry. Had he really not remembered the harsh things he had *just* told me? Or was this a trick?

"Darling, what's wrong?" He set a hand on my right shoulder, trying to get an explanation out of me.

"Do you not remember what you *just* said?" I yelled, turning to face him for the first time since I…

"Fell asleep," He finished my thought, holding a hand up to my cheek, wiping the tears away. "It was just a bad dream, love. I *promise* you." He kissed my forehead and took the bag from my grasp, setting it down on the floor as he picked me up in his arms, my legs wrapping around his waist.

"I'm so sorry-" I whispered.

"No, *I'm* sorry. I shouldn't have tried to make you sleep." He wrapped his arms so tightly around me that I didn't want him to *ever* let go.

"It's okay," I began, "Sleep feels amazing, you should try it. Really," I muttered into his shirt, the tears falling freely from my eyes.

"Don't cry, please, darling." He whispered, sitting down on the bed, me still in his lap wrapped tightly around him. "I have food for you. I thought that since food still tasted like food you could try and eat something. If you want, of course."

I could hear the worry in his voice, the worry that came from my reaction to my dream. He moved his hands to my blonde hair, smoothing it out and knotting his fingers in it as I sobbed quietly into his shirt.

"I'm sorry..." I apologized, making him shake his head slightly.

"It's alright, cry all you need, I'm here for you." He kissed my ear, making my body shiver in surprise.

After a while of sitting in his lap crying, I lifted my head and looked at the tray of food he had made for me, closing my eyes. Steam came off of the food when I reopened my eyes, proving my manifestation had worked!

"Woah-" I replied, getting off of Felix's lap and picking up the tray. I looked down at it for a second and then extended my arms out, the tray still in my hands. "Look! I did it!" I smiled brightly as he smiled and took the tray from me, wrapping me in a hug.

"Good job, try to move the bouquet of flowers to the bedside table without touching them." He instructed and I nodded after he let go of me.

I concentrated my mind on the bouquet of roses, picturing them in a white, sleek vase, sitting on the bedside table with a picture of me and Felix at prom in a matching frame to the mirror. I opened my eyes and saw the roses in a *clear* vase, the same one I had pictured, just clear. There was a photo of me and Felix sitting next to it, a beautiful photo we had taken at prom under the 'welcome' arch back earlier this year.

"Hey! You did it! You just didn't close your eyes for long enough so the vase didn't finish, but you did it!" I looked at him and then back at the vase that he now replaced with the sleek white one I had envisioned.

We spent a little bit longer on my manifesting abilities and then he asked me to try the food he had made, and I happily did.

"This is amazing, Felix! Who knew you could cook so well?" I smiled brightly, pushing the fork back into the fluffy buttermilk pancakes he had made.

"Can you believe that I didn't manifest it?" He chuckled, manifesting the cookbook he had used to make this spectacular meal. "I used this. You always trust women's *cookbooks*." He smiled, vanishing the cookbook back downstairs.

I reached for the glass of chocolate milk he had manifested when he manifested the cookbook in his hands.

"I made that, too. I just forgot it downstairs." He climbed into the bed with me, sitting next to me. I took a long sip of the rich chocolate drink, savoring the flavors as soon as it reached my tongue.

"Oh my god, Felix-" I looked at him and smiled. He reached a hand up to my face and wiped the chocolate from my mouth with his thumb.

"There," He whispered, moving the tray off of my lap and kissing me, smiling against my lips. I smiled and flushed, kissing him back.

"I really want to finish this food, it's amazing," I told him as we pulled away and he nodded, moving away from me.

"You can expect more of this, my love." He got up and walked to the computer on the glass desk. He sat down and did some work as I ate and watched the TV that was on the tan stand in front of the bed, playing some random house renovating show.

After I finished eating I walked over to Felix and stood behind him, my chin on his head. He spun his chair around, facing me as I turned around and sat down on his lap. He laughed but turned the chair back around to the desk and wrapped his arms around me, still doing his work. I lay back against him and watched as he filled out a document for our new house.

"What does our house look like?" I asked, turning my eyes to meet him as he did as well.

"It's a cottage, kind of like Francis and Alice's, just… smaller." I smiled, "It's in the woods just because we might need to use the extra space for practicing and stuff. It has an attic and a basement. I was thinking we could use the attic for magic-related things, and the basement-"

"'*Magic-related things'?*" I cut him off, furrowing my eyebrows.

"I can teach you when we get to our house, don't worry." He smiled, looking back at his monitor.

"What else were you going to say?" I asked, sorry that I cut him off.

"I was thinking we could use the basement for music stuff, just because I'd love to have a place where I can make more music for you." I flushed, just thinking of Felix in a room full of records, CDs, instruments, and music-making equipment.

"I think that'd be great. I'd love for you to have a place where you can just be surrounded by music." I smiled, kissing his cheek and getting up off his lap.

He continued doing the document for our house for the majority of the day as I was just checking my social media apps and texting Jenny, Harley, and Alex. He finished up and joined me in bed, laying next to me and taking my phone.

"Hey!" I smiled, leaning in to kiss him as he set my phone down on the bed.

"I'm better to look at than a screen." He repositioned himself so he was hovering over top of me.

He kissed me on the lips but then moved to my jaw and neck, making a small moan release from my lips. He chuckled, looking up at me through his eyebrows as he continued kissing my neck.

"Sleep time~" He hummed, moving himself to my side and sitting up.

"Fine," I grumbled, positioning myself to set my head on his chest. I looked over at the clock, *8:23 pm.* Why were we going to bed so early?

"Because we've gotta get up early, pack, go to your house, and drive the 12 hours there. Plus I wanted to give you time to say goodbye to your parents." He smiled, rubbing his hand over my messy hair, trying to make sense of it.

"Alright," I smiled too, closing my eyes and falling asleep.

I didn't dream that night, I just fell asleep, and then woke up. I looked at the clock that read; *7:04.* I woke up a lot *earlier* than I wanted to, but crawled out of bed and walked downstairs, realizing that my t-shirt and shorts I wore yesterday had been switched out for a manifested lace gown, not as revealing as the one I've worn previously.

"Hey," I said as I walked into the kitchen, being met with Felix cooking and packing at the same time.

"Hey, love," He didn't look up but a smile formed on his face.

"Whatcha makin'?" I smiled back, resting my head on his left shoulder and peering at the delicious-smelling food he was cooking.

"Food," He replied, nodding over at the cookbook that was resting on the counter. I peered over at the cookbook page and saw that he was attempting to make an omelet.

"You're doing it wrong," I informed, moving my head off him and standing next to him, one hand on my hip, the other on his shoulder.

"How so? I'm following the steps." He looked at me, his face flushed a little.

"You didn't season the eggs." I nodded at the salt and pepper still sitting in the spice carousel.

"It didn't say to add it," He frowned, looking down at his omelet.

"Most cookbooks just assume the person making it knows already or is going to eat it with salsa." I shrugged, grabbing the salt out and pouring some into the mixture of eggs he already had made, leaving the one on the stove unseasoned.

"Always trust a woman." He chuckled, calling back to when he said always trust a woman's *cookbook*. I smiled, moved to the island, and sat down on one of the tan stools.

"How far away is our house from the college?" I asked,

"About ten minutes," He said as he concentrated on the food.

"Alright," I looked over at the TV in the living room and closed my eyes, manifesting it to be on and playing another episode of the house flipper show that was playing last night. Felix chuckled at my laziness, causing me to laugh.

After I ate Felix's delicious omelets, he told me to pack whatever I wanted from the room upstairs and then flashed away to do something. I walked up the stairs and flashed to our closet, picking out the shirts, pants, nightgowns, and other various things I wanted and/or needed.

When I was done packing I made the bed, opened the curtains, signed out of the computer, sprayed the bathroom, and closed the door, trying to make less work for the maid. I walked downstairs and sat down on the couch, pulling my phone out of my back pocket and calling Mom.

"Everything alright?" She asked.

"Yeah, I just wanted to let you know Felix and I are going to be stopping over to pick up my stuff soon."

"You're leaving already?" I could tell the smile she had faded down into a frown, but I think it was just a coincidence that I could tell because I know her so well.

"Yeah, remember how we wanted to leave right after summer started?" I reminded, looking at Felix as he walked in the door with some more elixir.

"Yeah, I remember." She said, her voice still sad. Felix pointed to the door, letting me know he'll be outside. I nodded and he closed the door.

"Good. We'll be there in a little bit to pick up my stuff."

"Alright, see you soon." She hung up and I set my phone down, grabbed my messenger bag and the two other bags that sat on the floor of the living room, walked outside, and locked the door, handing the keys to Felix.

"Ready?" Felix asked, opening the trunk of his Volvo and grabbing the bags from me as I nodded.

"I want that one by me, please." I requested and he nodded, putting the other bags in the trunk and closing the door tightly. He sped around the car and opened my door for me, flashing to his side in seconds.

He started the engine and looked over at me as I nodded, telling him to drive away from this amazing, tropical palace.

We got to my parents' house in about ten minutes, pulling into the driveway and flashing out of the car as I knew my parents weren't watching.

"Why do I know that they aren't looking? I also knew that my mom had a smile that faded when I told her we were leaving Haines."

"Good sense I guess, we can try to talk to Francis about it."

"Oh right- Didn't Francis ask us to stay here until we had what was wrong with me sorted out?" I asked, worried that we were doing the opposite of what Francis had asked of us.

"Yes and no. I talked to him about us just manifesting ourselves back to him and he said that it doesn't matter to him. I wanted to get us in this house before our three-year anniversary tomorrow." He smiled, holding my hand as we walked up to the door. He knocked yet I just opened it, welcoming ourselves in.

Mom ran up, her mascara slightly smudged, showing she had been crying. She gave me a big hug and then turned to Felix, smiling when she gave him a hug, too. Dad walked up, hugging me and shaking Felix's hand. We said hello and then went up to my room and started packing.

"I'm gonna miss this room." I frowned slightly but smiled when Felix put a hand under my chin, turning me to face him.

"You're gonna *love* what we did with your room at *our* house." He smiled, leaning in and kissing me.

We packed my things together and stopped when we had to pack my record player and records. Felix suggested that we leave it here since he has a lot of them, but since I got it a couple of weeks after Felix and I started dating, I packed it in a hard bag that Felix had made for me to carry the record player in. We put away the rest of Felix's clothes that were in my closet and dresser, that being the last thing we had to pack.

Felix and I said goodbye to Mom and Dad and promised to come back before summer was over. Felix and I got into his car and looked back at my house.

"You ready?" He asked as I nodded, holding his hand over the middle column. "Okay,"

He smiled, turning the engine on as I continued looking back at my parents waving us goodbye. Tears stung my eyes and I did my best to keep them back, but a couple of them managed to fall from my eyes.

"It's alright, cry all you need, love." He looked at me, wiping the tears from my cheeks with his thumb.

We stopped at the *'Welcome to Haines, Alaska'* sign that was on the outside of Haines, right when you entered or exited. We looked at it for a second, and then Felix kept driving, leaving our life in Haines behind.

Seventeen

The drive was long and boring, yet full of funny and cute moments. Felix and I stopped at a coffee shop, bought some souvenirs, and got some *delicious*-tasting coffee.

"This is so good!" I smiled, looking at Felix, wishing he could taste it too.

"Even if I *could* taste it, I don't like coffee." He smiled back, "That's probably just because I haven't had coffee in three-hundred years." He leaned back in his chair and folded his arms, watching me drink my coffee.

"Sad," I muttered, laughing along with him.

The barista looked over and I mouthed a *'sorry'* like I did as Caroline, spiking a memory in my brain.

"When can we visit the pavilion again?" I looked at him with desperate eyes.

"Soon, love. I promise." He reached his hand out across the table to hold mine, looking at me with his soft, caring, hazel eyes.

When we finally entered Fairbanks we went straight to our house. Felix had told me to close my eyes when we got to the private forest it was in. Apparently, Francis had done *more* than just get us a house, he got us an entire forest along with a river, right in our backyard. Felix pulled up to our house and I tried my hardest not to try and *sense* what it looked like.

"We're here. Keep your eyes closed." He instructed.

"Okay," I smiled, squinting my eyes harder and putting my hands over them.

He helped me out and brought me to the front of the house, facing the car to not spike my mind to go and figure out what it looks like.

"You ready?" I could hear his smile through his words. I nodded and he turned me around as I moved my hands and opened my eyes.

"Oh!" Was all I managed to get out as I just looked at the house, the green moss so vibrant, the dark wood enchanting. "I-It's beautiful!" I turned to face Felix, our smiles both so wide.

"Wait 'til you see the inside." He took my hand and walked us up to the large curved door. He inserted a black key and turned the handle, opening the door and motioning for me to go first.

I walked inside and was met with bright colors like my room back home had been. There was a spiral staircase that came down from the basement and led up to the attic. Lots of roses were around the house, in the form of pillows, paintings, actual roses, and a floor lamp in the foyer.

The open arch in front of me led to the kitchen, which led to the dining room. There was an arch to my left that led to the living room, and then there was a tall, dark door that led to the bedroom.

"Isn't it amazing?" Felix asked, sliding an arm around my waist.

"It really is…" I said as I looked around the foyer.

"Shall we look around?" He turned his gaze to me, looking at me with his soft, loving eyes. I nodded and he walked me into the living room first.

There was a big window in the room, looking out to the river and forest that surrounded the house. There was a big royal blue couch on one side and a red armchair on the other. The TV was placed in the big window with plants and art surrounding it. There were countless plants everywhere. There was one giant plant in the corner by the tv that took up a lot of space, yet was really cute. On the right wall, there was an opening that led to the dining room. There was a big multicolored, knit rug in the middle of the room, covering the beautiful hardwood floor, yet helping fill the space.

The dining room had a side table with two chairs, one red, and one orange. Along with a dark brown dining table in the middle of the room with four rustic, fancy chairs surrounding it. Underneath the table was a dusty pink rug with little roses following the outskirts of it, along with the tan circle rug that was under the two-person table. There were paintings, candles, and plants everywhere, making our house feel like a museum.

'Could there be any more old art?' I thought, chuckling to myself.

"Yes. Yes, there could, because there *is*." Felix responded, kissing the top of my head and laughing along with me and my thought.

He walked us back to the foyer and then to the kitchen which was on the opposite wall of the living room. The kitchen had dark counters and cabinets, along with a black sink, oven, and refrigerator. The space was small, yet fit together nicely. There were a lot of postcards from the early 1900s arranged messily on a bulletin board.

"Those postcards were all the notes and photos we exchanged back in the 1890s. They mean a lot to me, and eventually, I can show you the story of who you were, and how we met back in the early 1900s." He looked down at me, still clutched to his waist, and smiled as I grew happier at just the mention of visiting the pavilion.

If you counted how many different plants there were in our house, you'd be *surprised*. Felix told me that in our entire house, there were *2,300* plants used—(Not counting the plants that were in the garden out back).

If you counted how many different paintings of music or portraits Felix had from the 1600s to the 1900s—(Almost all of our art is of either roses, music, or old portraits/art)—you'd be *concerned*. There were a total of *1,928* art pieces around our house. Felix told me he wished he got 2 more, but they wouldn't have it anywhere other than the bathroom.

"It's crazy and excessive, I know, you don't need to tell me." He laughed, seeing my thought process as he told me the number of paintings and plants used.

He opened the door to the bathroom, and inside it was pretty small and basic, yet rich and enchanting. There was a fancy sink and toilet, but the best part was the giant, beautiful bathtub that was on the far wall of the slim room. There were yet more plants and art, just not as many as in the other rooms.

There was a door on the right wall that led to our bedroom and Felix went and opened it, pushing me inside and making me land on the bed. He positioned himself overtop of me and kissed my neck, causing me to blush, smile, and shiver as a wave of joy went down my spine.

"I'm so glad we have our own room, my love." He smiled, pausing to look up at me for a second.

"Me too," I smiled back brighter, reaching a hand down to his head, and running my fingers through his dark blond hair.

He moved us to lay down on the bed, me on top of him as he rubbed my back. He whispered things into my ears and hummed my song, smiling when my mind started to doze off.

"I love you, *Mon Soleil*," He said that thing in French again and kissed the top of my head as I fell asleep, the last words of his I heard echoing in my mind.

"Mon Soleil," He began in French, his voice so prominent it felt like I was reliving it again. "I love you, *Soleil*." He finished, his body hitting the cold lake below. No no no, this couldn't

be happening again. I knew Felix was safe, why was I still having this nightmare? Especially on a day like this, this amazing, exciting, and fun, yet tiring day.

"No, no no, Felix!" I yelled, waking up in a cold sweat. I looked around, Felix was nowhere to be seen, though.

"Stop acting like everything revolves around you. It doesn't." Harley's stern voice echoed around the dark room.

"Stop that…" I whispered, looking at the memories of Harley, Alex, Jenny, Michael, and I that were plastered around the dark void of my mind.

"Why? Are you afraid to admit that you've left us for Mr. '*Tall, tan, and handsome*'?" Jenny mocked, memories of Felix popping up, covering over the memories of me and my friends.

"Carmen. You're so selfish. You'd rather spend time hanging with Felix than you would with us, your *childhood* friends." Alex's voice raised, causing tears to form in my eyes.

"I'm sorry…" I muttered, feeling as small as could be. Wishing I *was* as small as could be.

"It's too late for that." I saw a new, vivid memory, a memory of Harley, Jenny, and Michael all leaving me. All because of *Felix.*

"Goodbye, Carmen." Alex looked back at me and walked away, following behind everyone else.

"No, please don't go!" I hollered, just to be ignored as they walked off, disappearing into the fog. The tears fell from my eyes like rivers, falling and not stopping until they trailed off my face. I woke up and was met with a worried Felix, who I was still in the grasp of.

"Carmen, it's alright, you're okay." Felix cooed, holding me tightly to his chest, not letting go. "I'm here, you're okay." He shushed as my sobs got louder.

"I-" I tried to talk but Felix shushed me again with a small peck to the lips, tucking my head into his chest as I cried.

"Shh~" He cooed, trying to make me feel safe and comfortable.

After a while of crying in Felix's grasp, my sobs stopped, my breath steadied, my mind relaxed.

"May I just ask if there was a reason for your nightmare tonight?" He has asked this question every time I've had a nightmare around him, but I never really had a clear answer. "I hope it wasn't me," He added, making me feel bad for what I was about to say.

"I-It was because of what you called me. You called me that when you were falling off the cliff… It just spiked a bad memory."

"*Mon Soleil*?" He asked, making me cringe. I nodded and he looked worried. "It means '*my sunshine*' in French, would you rather me call you '*mon amour*'? I think it's more fitting for you, my love." He smiled, trying to set the tone to love and happiness, not sadness and worry.

"Yeah… I love the name but I think that it'd be best to not call me that anymore." He nodded and sat up, me still in his lap.

"I understand that."

I set my head in the crook of his neck and exhaled deeply, collecting my thoughts. He rubbed my back and hummed my song, looking at the clock.

"It's two… I think you should try to go back to sleep."

"I don't want to have-" He cut me off.

"I'll be right here. If anything happens I won't make you sleep again. I promise," He grasped my waist and pushed me back from his neck, looking at my eyes.

"Okay… " I got off of his lap and laid down next to him as he repositioned himself to make space for my upper body in his lap.

I set my head on his chest, shifting myself to be more comfortable. He chuckled and I looked up at him, gazing into his amazing hazel eyes, almost getting lost in them.

"Goodnight, *mon amour*." He reached one of his hands out and moved the stray strand of hair in my face behind my ear.

I didn't have a nightmare after that, but I also don't remember having a dream. I woke up to me being placed on the bed, a note on the bedside table.

I'm out in the Kitchen, making breakfast. Don't worry, love.'

I set the note back down and sat up, looking at the paintings all over the walls. There was one larger painting that looked like Floyd and Francis, but I didn't pay attention to it. I bet that everyone in the 1700s looked the same.

I looked over at the clock, it read '*9:32*' I got out of bed and manifested the blankets and pillow to be set up neatly, making less work for me. I walked out to the kitchen and saw Felix making breakfast like he had said. He flashed over to me and wrapped an arm around my waist, setting his head on my shoulder

"Hey," He whispered, his voice echoing in my ear.

"Hi," I whispered back, "Whatcha making?" I peered over at the stove and he flashed in front of me, blocking my view.

"A secret three-year anniversary breakfast. Today is all about you, *amour,*" He kissed my forehead and smiled, wrapping his arm in mine. "Could you go sit in the living room as I prepare your breakfast, darling?" I nodded and he kissed my hand, letting go as I walked across the foyer and into the living room.

I lay down on the dark blue couch, the remote being manifested in my hand by Felix, who was looking around the arch at me, a big smile plastered on both of our faces. I set the remote on the floor and closed my eyes, relaxing my brain, but trying not to sleep.

About fifteen minutes later, Felix finished, announcing it as I got up and walked through the door on my left to the dining room, sitting at the two-person circle table, instead of the large six-person table.

"Here you go, love." He set my plates down in front of me, sitting across from me, a grin on his face.

"*All* of this?" I asked, looking down at the four plates of food he had prepared. He nodded and I took time to identify all of them.

There was a plate with two omelets, one with what looked like cupcakes or donuts, one with some… scones?... and one with a couple of waffles.

Felix laughed, "There are omelets, waffles, *Pain Au Chocolat*, and some *Chaussons aux Pommes*." He paused, awaiting my gaze to meet his. "Chaussons aux Pommes are just apple turnovers. It just translates to; 'Apple Pies'." He smiled.

"What about the *Pain Ow Choco-late*?" I asked, pronouncing it terribly.

"It's *Pain Au Chocolat,* love." He laughed softly, "Pain Au Chocolat is a French dish, most commonly served with tea or coffee. It's basically a croissant with chocolate inside. All it means is; 'Chocolate Bread'."

"Alright," Was all I said as I dug in, wanting to cheer Felix up by eating his French dishes first, and then eating the things I was used to.

"These are really good!" I smiled, eating a full piece of the chocolate bread.

"I know, right? I'm sad every day that I can't eat food." He kept his smile on his face as he said that, though.

"I wish you could. I'd introduce you to so many foods."

"I wish I could too, love."

The rest of the meal was quiet, I finished the French food and the waffles but stopped when

I got to the omelets. "What's wrong?" He asked, cocking his head.

"Did you season them this time?" I asked, crossing my arms playfully.

"Yes, I did." He smiled, manifesting the salt and pepper from the kitchen.

"Good," I smiled, cutting up the omelet and sticking a piece of egg into my mouth on my fork.

He set his hands on the table, folded softly. "Do they taste good?" I nodded, my face stuffed with food. "I'm glad," He smiled, leaning back and crossing his arms over his chest now.

I swallowed my food and coughed, the food going down wrong. "Sorry-" I said, covering my mouth with my hand.

"Why're you sorry?" He asked, stretching his arm out to reach my hand which was laying on the table in a fist.

"Habit, I guess. I don't like to be rude while eating."

I moved my hand away from my mouth and looked down at my lap, sensing his thoughts of *'Habit? Why? Did your parents shame you for choking?'* I shook my head and looked up, not meeting his gaze as I spoke.

"No. *I* don't like to be rude at the table. Whether that be choking or not." I explained, looking at him, my light blue eyes staring into his beautiful, irresistible hazel ones, not wanting to ever look away.

"Alright," He cleared his throat, "I don't mind it though," He rubbed the back of my hand with his thumb, comforting me although I didn't need it.

"Anyways, I'm done now, I'm going to go wash my plate, if that's okay." I stood up, brushing my pants off even though nothing was on them.

"Of course, you can, darling. I don't understand the meaning of you and your politeness." He got up too, taking my plate before I could, gesturing for me to walk to the kitchen.

"I guess I just feel out of place with you…" I murmured, focusing on my cuticles, not on Felix.

"Why?" He cocked his head and turned around, looking at me softly.

"You speak and act so politely. I think my body just has an instinct to do the same around you. I'm sorry-" He cut me off, his eyebrows furrowed slightly.

"You think I'm mad at you for acting like that? Love, I'm not upset with you. There is never a reason to *be* upset with you." He put his hand on the side of my face and rubbed my cheek, smiling when he realized I leaned into it.

"I see. You don't like when I act so formal around you." He set the plate on the table in the foyer and put his other hand on the other side of my face, pulling me closer and pushing our foreheads together. "You like me to be all loving and *not* formal."

By the way, he had said it. I thought he was mad, but he shook his head, reading my thoughts about the situation. He manifested a rose, it already wrapped tightly in my palm. He pulled out foreheads away but I tugged at the neck of his shirt, pulling him into a kiss.

Eighteen

"I love you, Carmen." He smiled, kissing down my neck and jaw.

"I love *you*, Felix." I smiled back, moaning softly as he bit down on my neck. He chuckled, going further down.

"Happy three years, *mon amour*."

He looked up at me, his hands unbuttoning the blue and white nightshirt I wore. After he got it undone, the rest of this night was our first moment like this in history and something I hope to visit in the pavilion in the future.

"Hi," I walked down the spiral stairs and stood behind him. He was sitting at his desk and putting together a song he's been working on for this very day.

"Hey, love" He smiled, looking back at me and making me straddle him. "Look," He said, setting his head on my shoulder and looking at the monitor that was on some music editing service.

"What's it about?" I asked, turning my head to kiss his temple, looking at the screen after.

"You." Was all he said, his smile still wide and bright, chuckling as I flushed a bright red. "You're cute," He turned his head, looking at me softly, holding his gaze for a while before blinking.

I didn't say anything, I just kept my eyes focused on him, refusing to look away until he did. Getting lost in his beautiful hazel eyes. He smiled and leaned in, pecking my nose and chuckling. He leaned away and looked at his monitor, turning it off and looking back at me.

He spun his chair around and stood up, me still being clutched to his waist tightly, barely holding on, being held up by his strong grasp on my back. He walked up the spiral stairs, turned off the lights, and brought me to the living room. He sat down on the blue couch, pulling me tightly to his chest.

"Do you want anything for lunch?"

He asked, muttering into my newly washed hair. I nodded and grabbed his phone out of his back pocket, pulling him away from me a little bit to see the screen. I put in the passcode, my birthday, '6-2-05', and opened *Doordash*.

"Whatcha ordering?" He peered at the phone, looking at all of the fast food restaurant names on the screen, watching my finger stop on a local burrito shop.

"Burritos," I smiled, placing an order for five burritos, pressing the toppings that I wanted on them, turning his phone off, and setting it down on the couch as I pushed my head into the crook of his neck, my hands sliding under his arms and holding his back tightly.

"Alright," I could sense his smile somehow.

We sat like that in silence for a while, just listening to each other's breathing, being held tightly to each other until we got interrupted by a knock at our door. I got up off of Felix's lap and headed for the door quickly, opening it and being met with a man who was about my age.

"I have an order for Carmen," He began, looking up from his order book and meeting my gaze. "O-oh, I-" He stuttered, clearing his throat. He leaned up against the doorframe and almost slipped, making a small laugh come out of my mouth.

"Sorry- I'm Daniel, your Doordasher. I must say this house is pretty fitting for a fine girl like you." And as soon as he said that Felix walked up to us, wrapping an arm around my waist. Daniel flushed instantly and straightened his standing position after seeing Felix.

"Thanks so much," Was all Felix said, grabbing the brown paper bag from Daniel's sweaty grasp and setting it on the purple ottoman.

"Y-yeah, no problem, sir." He cleared his throat again, his face getting redder. "Have a good day, ma'am... A-and you too, sir." He turned around awkwardly and walked to his car, his eyes grew wide as we watched him pull out of our drive.

"You didn't have to do that, y'know." I turned to face him, standing on my tippy toes when he leaned in.

"I didn't like some random guy flirting with you. Is it a crime to protect my beautiful girlfriend from some sweaty stranger?" He laughed, grabbing the bag from the ottoman and letting go of my waist, grabbing my hand instead and tugging me along to the dining room.

"Why do guys react like that? I'm not *that* pretty. Am I?" I asked, sitting down at the small table again.

"Yes, you are. You saw yourself, did you not?" I flushed, looking down at our interlocked hands that were set across the table.

"But I'm not, like, *that* pretty. Not pretty enough to make people get all flustered and stuff, right?" I looked up at him, my face hot with a bright crimson color spread across my cheeks. He chuckled, pulling my hand to his lips.

"Carmen, you are the prettiest woman I've ever laid my eyes on, I thought I told you this." He smiled warmly, enjoying the fact that I was so flustered.

"I didn't know if you were just saying that because you're my boyfriend or not…" I muttered, looking down.

"Carmen, even before you and I were dating I knew that you were the prettiest woman I've ever seen in all of my 300 years. I'm not just saying that because I'm your boyfriend. I'm saying that because it's *true*."

"But I don't really recognize myself… My face and body are different. I have no more pimples, my skin basically glows with the correct lighting, and everything is so bright." I felt terrible just saying that, I felt spoiled. I was *complaining* about looking like a goddess. Who in their right mind would think like this?

"How about we talk about this later? For now, you should eat." He looked at the brown paper bag that was on the table, reaching out to grab it as I placed my hand on top of his.

"I think you should try some, Felix. Maybe it's changed. Maybe you *can* taste food, you've just never done it since becoming immortal."

"Love," He tried to protest but I shook my head.

"Please? One bite. For me?" I looked at him softly.

"Fine, but only because I can't say no to you." He chuckled softly, pushing the paper bag to me.

I grabbed out two of the five burritos and slid one to Felix, smiling when he started to unwrap the aluminum foil. I unwrapped mine and waited for Felix to finish undoing his. He looked at me and I nodded reassuringly, trying to show him that even if it tasted like nothing, it was okay.

We took a bite at the same time, and thanks to my new immortal abilities, the flavor was overpowering compared to what I'm used to. Felix set his burrito down, chewing his food slowly as he opened his mind to me, allowing me to hear what he thinks of it.

'There's some flavor, but it's not much.' He thought, swallowing hard.

'It's alright. I promise. I just wanted to see if it was normal for immortals, and you just didn't know cause you never got hungry.' I smiled, taking another bite.

"It tastes good, I just didn't get much flavor."

He took my hand again, sliding the burrito to me, and grabbing his phone out of his pocket.

"Shit," He muttered under his breath, "It's Francis. Give me a second," He walked out of the dining room and to the living room. He walked faster than normal so I knew something was wrong.

When he came back he rubbed his temple, a neutral look was on his face. "What's wrong?" I asked as he sat down.

"Francis needs us back in Haines. He needs to figure out what *exactly* is wrong." He paused, biting the inside of his mouth. "The little burrito fiasco didn't help either. He read my thoughts when I opened them to you and found out what we were doing." He scratched his chin.

"Alright, when do we have to leave?" I grabbed my second burrito, the one Felix had tried, bit a chunk out of it, and got overwhelmed by the flavor *again*.

"We don't have to drive, darling." He chuckled softly, trying to change the mood. "We can just manifest ourselves there as we did to the pavilion." My face brightened when he said 'pavilion' but dimmed back down when I knew he wasn't talking about visiting today.

"I'm sorry, love." He squeezed my hand, "I promise we can go when we return." He smiled, standing up and letting go of my hand.

He walked up the stairs to the attic, our 'magic room', that I hadn't been allowed in prior. I stuffed the rest of my burrito in my mouth and then manifested the others to be in the fridge.

I followed him up the stairs and was met with a dark room, illuminated by the candles placed on random shelves and tables. There was a big rose carpet, like the one at the house Francis and Alice had lent to us, just a black rose, not a bright red one.

"Come here," He extended his hand out, pulling me close to him. "Close your eyes and focus," I did what he had instructed and dropped my hand from his.

"Imagine a veil of light—like the one you saw before we got to the pavilion—in *this* case, is Francis and Alice's house. Imagine yourself in my old room, landing on my bed, with me beside you."

His eyes were closed too, his left hand balled tightly in a fist, his face calm, relaxed, yet on the inside, he was worried. I don't know why, but this information I couldn't see waved through me as if I touched the front of a book, being able to know the beginning, middle, and end of the story, no matter what.

I did what he said. I envisioned myself walking through the white veil of light, landing on Felix's bed, and being at Francis and Alice's house, in Felix's old bedroom. I opened my eyes and was met with what I had imagined, just a little more detailed than my imagination had been.

Felix's room was mainly empty other than a bunch of extra records and CDs he had on his shelf, along with a photo of me and him for our *two*-year anniversary.

"Hey," He smiled, laying on his side with his hand under his head.

"Hi," I flushed, smiling back.

"Carmen? Felix?" Francis knocked, awaiting an answer.

"Yeah?" Felix asked, getting up off the bed and taking my hand to follow.

"May I come in?" Felix just opened the door and walked out into the hallway, me following too.

Francis brought us back to his work room and asked me to sit down on the bed in the middle of the room again. I obeyed and sat on the bed, Felix sitting in the light gray armchair next to me.

"So, I was looking at the scan we took, and I thought it'd be best to try and figure out what you ate the day before you became immortal."

"I'll try and remember…" I looked down at my nails, picking at the chipped red nail polish I wore.

"If you can't remember everything that's okay. I just need to know what big meals or something you had on the fourth." He grinned, his face a perfect representation of calm.

"Uhm…" I looked at Felix and he shrugged, not remembering either. "I had lunch at school that day, went here, had a cookie, and then drank the elixir by accident. After that, all I had was some soup when I got home because I was so thirsty and everything looked brighter than normal." I explained, my eyes back on my nails, chipping at my nail polish again.

"Then I'm not sure if I can say it was the food's fault..." He frowned, turning to his monitor.

Nineteen

We spent quite a while at Francis and Alice's house, trying to find out *why* I was like this.

Francis settled on; "We will have to do more tests. In the meantime, I'm going to try and do some more studies on immortals, and maybe use you two as examples." He explained as Felix and I walked to Felix's old room, getting ready to return home.

"Thank you, Francis. We can come back anytime you need us." Francis nodded and Felix and I walked the rest of the way to Felix's room, Francis stopping in the hallway, watching us leave.

"Are we just going back home?" I asked, taking Felix's hand when he opened his old bedroom door.

"I have someplace I want to take you. It's only four and I think this would be perfect." He smiled, closing his eyes, which signaled for me to do the same.

He visioned a perfect field of roses, the sun shining brightly over us, but not too hot. He made a red and white picnic blanket appear in the field. Sandwiches and other various foods are placed in a basket on the blanket.

And like that, we were already out of Francis's house, out of Haines, and in Fairbanks, in an amazing flower field in our backyard

"Oh my god-" I covered my mouth as I saw the flower field. I was standing next to Felix, just looking at the marvelous red and pink rose field. Felix grabbed my hand and tugged me onto the red and white picnic blanket.

"It fits you perfectly, love."

He smiled, pulling me on top of him, sitting on his lap. He leaned in and placed a kiss on my nose, chuckling when I tilted my head down and kissed his lips, our mouths fit perfectly together, being made for each other.

"You're perfect," He smiled, kissing my forehead softly.

"Says you-" I muttered, smiling with him.

"Says me,"

He laid back and I fell with him, landing harshly on his chest. He chuckled and held me close, asking if I was okay as he kissed my head. I nodded although my heart was practically beating out of my chest.

How did I get so lucky? I thought, pushing my head into his neck harder, trying to hide my flushed face. He pulled the back of my shirt up, showing my pale skin, and rubbed my back, being careful around a scar I still have from *that* night.

We sat like that for a while, but he finally sat back up, moving me off of his lap. He reached for the picnic basket and handed it to me, smiling at my still, very bright, red face. I pulled out some sandwiches, two cake slices, orange juice, various berries, and a salad.

"I wasn't sure what you wanted, so I just manifested this. If you'd rather have something else I can…" He began, stopping when he saw me bite into one of the ham, cheese, and lettuce sandwiches. He grinned, pushing the hair out of my face and behind my ear.

"This is really good!" I smiled, taking another big bite of the sandwich.

"That makes sense… I didn't make it-"

"Your cooking is great, Felix." He didn't believe me, "You can't say it's not. The last time you tried your own cooking was the 1700s, so don't even." I assured him, making him look up at me.

"That may be true but I can tell it isn't *that* good." He still had that bright, happy smile plastered on his face, proving he wasn't trying to start an argument.

"It is!" I said too fast, making him believe me less than he did earlier.

"I know you think that, but compared to *Gordan Ramsey*? I'd look like a fool!" He chuckled at his joke, and the fact he knew I was picturing Gordan Ramsey calling him an *'idiot sandwich'*.

"A hot fool," I corrected, making him blush a light pink.

I was glad that these 'immortal eyes' could see the small amount of pink he had on his cheek because there was *no* way that human eyes could see it if my eyes barely could.

After I finished eating, Felix made the picnic things go away in a second, just having us stay in the flower field, laying in the small patch of grass the blanket had been laid in.

"Y'know, I thought we could go to an arcade. Like we did on our first date." He smiled, pulling me onto his lap. I flushed instantly, remembering our first date and how we fell in love.

"Felix! Look! It looks just like you~" I teased, holding out an orange cat with a dark orange spot around its eye, as a matching brown cat with a light brown spot was tucked under my armpit.

"Thanks, Carmen," He smiled, taking the cat from me and giving the guy behind the counter the tickets for our matching cats.

"Do we have to leave yet?" I asked, looking back at the arcade games.

"No, love, we don't." He snaked an arm around my waist, making me blush instantly.

"What did you call me?" I murmured.

"Love," he answered, pausing for a second, "Would you rather me not call you that?" He asked, his face calm and caring.

"No," I sucked my teeth, "I like it..." I admitted, blushing brighter.

"I'm glad," He tugged me along to a claw machine with *Squishmallows* in it that we spent forever trying to win.

We spent a couple more hours in the arcade, laughing, smiling, and sharing our first kiss in front of the claw machine when he finally won. We had a romantic night, a romantic *first date*. He was amazing, both personality and looks wise.

"Carmen~" Felix laughed, waving a hand in front of my face, laughing harder when I opened my eyes and shook my head, blushing at the sight of his happy, relaxed face.

"Sorry..." I looked at him, my face hot.

"Whatcha thinking about there, love?" He smiled.

"Our first date…" I looked down at my fingernails, picking at the nail polish that was left over.

"I knew it!" He chuckled.

"You- How?" I questioned, furrowing my eyebrows.

"You were deep in thought when I said I was thinking of taking you to an arcade. It was kinda easy to figure out, Carmen," He chuckled again, closing his eyes and manifesting us to the arcade.

The arcade was lit up nicely by all of the games and stuff that were around the room. There were only two other people in the building, eating pizza and chatting.

"After this, I have somewhere special I want to take you," He smiled, tugging my arm to the front counter,

"Ah! Felix and Carmen! How are you two doing on this fine evening?" The British man behind the counter named Jaxson asked as a wide, toothless smile spread across his face.

"It's our three-year anniversary and I thought we'd visit before we go back to

Fairbanks." Felix's face stayed blank, and his tone didn't seem like he was happy to see Jaxon.

"How lovely!" Jaxon smiled wide, showing his bright white teeth.

Jaxon was flawless, there was no doubt about it. He had no acne, super bright teeth, amazing green eyes, plump, pink lips, and more. As I was thinking about it my face must have looked confused.

"Carmen, you alright?" Felix asked, squeezing my hand harder, making my mind jump out of whatever it was doing. I nodded and he furrowed his eyebrows. "You sure? We don't have to be here if you don't want to. Are you *thirsty*?" He asked, pulling a metal flask that had the elixir in it out of his leather jacket pocket.

"No..." I continued to look up at Jaxon, not able to take my eyes off of him. Jaxon just smiled more, cocking his head at the situation, his eyes on mine.

"Do we need to leave?" Felix asked, *'She better not do anything bad.'* He thought, his grasp tightening on my hand.

"I think so..." I whispered back, blinking but still not able to keep my eyes off Jaxon.

"Can I help you, Carmen?" Jaxon chuckled, his gaze still on mine but his face not friendly.

"We have to leave." Felix began, looking up at Jaxon, tugging me along. "She doesn't feel well…" He lied, his voice was stern as he said goodbye and walked out the door with me in front of him.

"Stay safe! Wouldn't want her to come to me." Jaxon chuckled and Felix muttered a swear word under his breath.

"What happened in there?" He asked calmly as he walked us across the street to an empty parking lot.

"I…" I began, "I don't know…" I looked at my fingers, my face red from embarrassment. "Are you mad?" I didn't mean for the words to slip out, but I'm kind of glad they did.

"No," He paused, reached a hand out, and moved my chin so I was looking at him. Getting lost in his amazing hazel eyes. "Why would you think that, darling?" His other hand held mine, rubbing circles on my pale skin.

"I-" I stopped, tears forming in my eyes.

"Is something wrong, love?" He asked, bringing my hand up to his mouth.

"I'm just really emotional for some reason." I stopped, looking at him, "I'm sorry."

"You have no need to be sorry. It's okay."

He smiled a warm, caring smile, looking at me for another second and then turning to the windshield.

"How about we visit the pavilion? I would like to show you how it was before I confessed my love… And if you prove ready for it… after." He closed his eyes and manifested us at the pavilion, me right next to him.

"I love you," I said as I snuggled into his lap after being manifested on the couch in the pavilion.

"*Je t'aime*, Carmen" He smiled, wrapping an arm around me and pulling me closer to him.

Twenty

"Felix, could you be a doll and get the door for me? Caroline is sleeping and she deserves somewhat of a break," Madame Bridget, an incredibly rich, English-speaking woman in France, asked, sitting on the couch eating from a golden bowl of strawberries.

"Yes, Ma'am," Sir Felix replied, opening the front door and getting the newspaper as soon as she asked.

Sir Felix was Madame Bridget's adopted child. He stayed with her even though he was 18 years old and previously emancipated. I, however, was their family's maid. I did what they asked, with no hesitation. That's why she let me sleep for that extra time that morning.

I didn't sleep in a closet, or on a spare couch, I had a room. One of their pantries, that is. It was a decently sized space but had no door, so there was a curtain draped over the entry, not blocking out noise or light.

Whenever I wasn't working I was instructed to find something to do or to sit in my room with the curtain closed as Madame Bridget and Sir Felix watched the television. It was different when just Sir Felix or the butlers were home, though. Most of the time, when Sir Felix was alone in the house with me, he invited me to watch the television, to just call him *Felix* and even whispered things in French to me that I didn't understand as much as I once had.

"*Tu es magnifique aujourd'hui.*"

He said to me, moving the lock of hair that was in my face behind my ear. I could only make out one of the words, *magnifique*, which means magnificent or beautiful. Had *Sir Felix* called *me* beautiful?

"I-" I tried to speak but my throat tightened, not allowing me to speak or move or anything.

"It's alright," He responded, moving away from me as he thought I was uncomfortable.

"I'm sorry Sir Felix… I'm not uncomfortable… I'm-"

"No, it's alright. You're flustered. I understand you don't know how to react. I truly *do* understand, *Caroline.*"

That was one of the first times I had heard him call me that. He normally had to call me maid when I worked around his mother, and if we were alone he just called me *amour*. I knew it was French, yet I couldn't figure out what it *meant*.

He reached over the side of the beautiful armchair he had moved to and grabbed a glass full of some red liquid.

"What *is* that?" I asked, adding; "If I may ask." after I thought what I had said sounded rude and uncalled for.

"It's a medicine." He responded, taking a sip of the sparkly, deep red drink. "It helps me have stable blood sugar." He smiled, looking at me with his soft, hazel eyes.

"May I try it?" I asked, sort of regretting it when the words slipped out of my mouth. "I'm sorry, I shouldn't have asked that..." I murmured afterward.

"No, it's alright. I am truly sorry, but I cannot give you a sip of this." He set the glass back down on the table, looking at it and keeping his hand on the rim, even though it was set down.

"It's alright, I shouldn't have asked."

"It's okay, *amour.*" He smiled, looking back at me.

Suddenly, the scene changed and I was no longer in the brightly lit mansion.

Instead, I was outside, in a dark, deep alleyway, standing against a wall. A man across from me held a flintlock pistol in his hand and pointed it at me as my arms were tied above me to a pole that extended out of the side of the bakery that was next to us.

"I'm sorry, Caroline, but too many people love you. I can't risk anyone taking your life to become a..." He didn't finish his sentence, "Nevermind," He added and his strong British accent rang in my ears, making me forget he was about to *kill* me.

"May I get your name before I die?" I asked calmly, my voice relaxed and prepared for the inevitable.

"I can't tell you. In case you come back. But just so you know, you *can't* escape me, Caroline. We are *meant* to be together." He stepped forward into the light that was shining from the pole I was tied to.

"I'm meant to be with Sir Felix." My voice was nothing but a hoarse whisper.

"You're meant to be with me. You'll see sooner or later, *my love.*"

He finished his sentence and then the loud shot of the bullet shocked my ears, ringing as I felt blood trickle down my leg where he had shot. The rope untied and my body fell to the floor, landing in a pile of my own blood. The warm, thick, crimson liquid came out fast as he shot my right shoulder.

Suddenly, I wasn't in my body anymore, I was standing outside, staring at the bloody scene. A group of men all dressed in black walked through the alleyway, Sir Felix following behind them.

Felix rushed up to the scene, "Caroline…" He held my dead body's hand in his own. "No, No… Caroline…" He wept, kissing my bloody skin.

He stayed there for a while and one of the men dressed in black grabbed the flintlock, putting it into a small little bag.

"I'll see you in the next life, *mon amour*. I promise you that." He closed my eyes with his warm fingers and then set a kiss on my forehead.

I got out of the scene and turned to Felix, he looked at me, his face calm and soft. "I didn't mean for that scene to play… I'm sorry…" He apologized.

"It's alright. Really." I said, straddling his lap as his fingers moved to play with my soft blonde hair.

"I just want you to know… I did in fact follow you. In almost every one of your lifetimes. A couple of them a *certain someone* got to you first, and wouldn't allow me past their bodyguards."

"Who was it?" Felix looked down at my hands and removed his fingers from my hair, using one of his hands to interlock ours, and the other gripped my shirt. "Sorry…"

"It's alright. It's just… I can't exactly tell you. It'll cause a lot of-" I started coughing a lot, cutting him off.

He manifested the elixir and a cup of water, he held both out in front of me and I took the water. I couldn't stop coughing to take a sip.

"You alright?" He asked, still holding the elixir in front of himself. I nodded and kept coughing. Had I choked on air? I opened my mind and shared my thoughts with him.

'Everything is getting dark. Bring me to Francis.' Felix immediately grabbed my hand and manifested us in Francis' workroom. Francis ran in and saw me leaning up against his counter, a hand on my heart while the other was resting on Felix's knee.

"What happened?" He asked Felix.

"I don't know. One minute she was perfectly fine, the next she was coughing like crazy." He explained, pulling me up and placing me on the sleek black bed.

I leaned back and everything started spinning. Getting darker. Like the world was choosing for me to die now, instead of living a life of immortality.

I held a hand up to Felix and he pushed it tightly to his chest and knelt down next to me, kissing my pale skin, *tears* forming in his eyes.

"I love you," I managed to choke out before everything went black.

Felix - Twenty-One

Carmen was lying peacefully on the bed, her heart still pumping blood, but slowly. I don't even know what happened. Did her body have enough of fighting against the elixir? Was she destined to die every time I got close to her? Was *I* bad for her? Was karma to blame after I stole…

Francis cut off my thoughts, looking at me before he unbuttoned Carmen's shirt, exposing the blue lacy bra she wore. I nodded and he continued, placing his stethoscope on her heart, trying to listen for the faint beating that I could somehow hear from here, standing on the opposite side of the room, not being able to see Carmen like this.

"I can barely hear it. Can you listen and tell me the beating patterns?"

He asked, taking off his stethoscope and trying to hand it to me, but I waved it away, walking up to Carmen—my forever lover. My *soulmate,* as she had phrased it—laying on the bed, her heart barely beating.

I placed my hand on her heart and laid my head on her chest, listening to the very faint beating of her poor little heart.

"It's slow, but beating," I said, taking my head off of her chest. What had she *done* to deserve this? What did *I* do?

"Thank you, Felix." Francis smiled, trying to cheer me up, but it didn't work. I nodded and went back to standing over by the counter, texting Carmen's parents.

Me: Carmen is here and okay. Her heart is beating, but not as good as it should be. If we need to we can take her to the hospital, but I just wanted to let you know that she is okay.

Ana: What happened?

Me: She just had a coughing episode and then passed out. Francis and I are taking care of it.

Ana: Is Francis skilled enough to deal with her *heart*?

Chris: Take her to a hospital! I'm *not* okay with my daughter getting work done by some fake doctors!

Me: I assure you, Francis is not a *'fake'* doctor. He has moved through almost every specialty there is when it comes to doctors. He is more than capable of taking care of Carmen.

Chris: Well, it's not like I can stop you.

Ana: Just, please take good care of her, and if anything happens text us *immediately.*

Me: I will. I have to go now. I assure you she is safe and in good care. We won't do anything to harm her.

I turned off my phone and exhaled hard, causing Francis to look up at me. "Everything alright?" He asked and I nodded, looking at Carmen, her breathing spiking back up very faintly.

"Yeah, just…" I paused, walking back up to Carmen. I placed my head on her chest again, hearing *very* faint breathing. "She's *breathing*." I looked up at Francis, shock on both of our faces.

"That's good!" Francis said, as he turned to his cabinet and grabbed out a breathing bag, handing it to me.

I placed the bag over Carmen's mouth and pressed the ball, pushing air into her lungs. Her breathing quickened by a little bit, giving me *hope*.

Francis and I did that for a while, calling out her stats and what her BPM and such were. We took turns with the bag, me mainly keeping my fingers on her neck, trying to feel her heartbeat.

After about 10 minutes of doing that, we stopped as her BPM only rose up 2, proving that her heart was so worn down that it didn't even speed up as air was moving through her at a fast rate.

"I don't know what else to… Wait! Francis, do you have the elixir at least started? We could try and finish it as fast as possible." I stood up and turned to Francis.

"It's barely started…" He looked at his desk, the herbs and flowers spread across it. "Plus I don't have any human blood right now, nor the herbs that are necessary to make the elixir. They only bloom once a year." He turned back to me, looking at me with sad eyes, showing how much he knew this hurt me.

I looked back at Carmen. I wondered what she was experiencing but was too hurt already, so I didn't peer into her mind. Just sensing she was in the *Dark Realm*, even if she wasn't dead.

The Dark Realm was a place where immortals went when they died. The Dark Realm made everyone watch their past, no matter if they've been alive for thousands of years.

I've been there once, and not because I died, but because I *made* myself go there. I *forced* myself to go there because I couldn't bear the fact that Caroline—at the time—had died. So I sent myself there, refusing to let go of Caroline and my memories with her.

But then, after I spent about a year in my memories, I stopped, bringing myself out of the Dark Realm and going to meet Chloe—Caroline reincarnated.

Every time Carmen reincarnated she was 17 years old, every time *but* her life as Carmen, that is.

I'm not exactly sure why her life as Carmen was different, but then again, I don't know why in all her other lives she came back as a 17-year-old.

I *am* sure why she died. In every one of her lifetimes, she had before she became Carmen, she was killed. By someone we know now, I'm just not sure *who*.

"Felix!" Francis shook my arm, stopping me from thinking of what *could* be wrong. "Are you going to help me try and fix up a temporary elixir or are you just going to stand there?" He asked, walking to his desk and sitting in the black office chair that was behind it.

"Yeah... Sorry," I replied, walking up to the opposite side of the desk and skimming my fingers over the books that were on his 'magic shelf.'

The books on that shelf consisted of spells, potions, life, abilities, and elixir books. I pulled one off titled *'Elixirs: A Guide to Immortality'*, a book that Francis wrote back when he made elixirs all the time. Almost all the books on that shelf were written by Francis or Floyd.

"Page three-oh-seven." He told me, the pages in the book instantly flipping to that page.

My eyes grew wide, "Thanks," I said, and he nodded, looking at the pot he had on the table along with some herbs and flowers.

"Hey, Felix?" I looked up with a hum, "Do you think we could try using Carmen's blood? I'm thinking it'll work the same since her heart is still beating." He asked, grabbing a book off the shelf titled; *'Immortal Features',* written by him.

"If you think it'll work, I don't have a problem with it," I told him, looking at the page that was open.

Step One: Add the herbs listed below to a Mortar and Pestle, grind lightly, and wait until the herbs get mixed together nicely.

Step Two: Add lily of the valley, roses, coneflower, *natural* aroma, lemongrass, and potassium nitrate, and mix them together vigorously.

Step Three: Add 1 pint of human blood and half a pint of animal blood—carnivore blood works best—and mix together, adding

Step Four: Let sit in a pot or glass container for 2 hours. Mix once afterward, and drink.

"Alright, would you mind getting some for me please?"

"Sure," I stood up and grabbed a blood bag out of the cabinet along with a needle and a rubber tie.

I walked up to Carmen and lifted her arm up, wrapping the rubber band around her upper arm to stop the blood flow for a second. I got the blood bag situated and then pulled the protective casing off of the needle, inserting it into her arm softly.

I knew how Carmen was afraid of needles and taking blood, but this would do her good, it was *worth* it.

I got a little bit more than a pint and then stopped, putting a bandaid on her arm and throwing the needle away, along with the blue rubber gloves Francis had manifested me to wear before I began.

I took the bag off of the pole and walked over to Francis, putting the bag in his mini-fridge and sitting back down.

"Got enough?" Francis asked, flipping the page in his book. I nodded and looked back at the steps, manifesting the proper flowers and herbs, since I *could* manifest those, why wouldn't I take advantage of my abilities at that moment?

Felix - Twenty-Two

We finished the elixir the next night, forty-two hours after Carmen had had her coughing episode. The only thing we were missing were those flowers that only bloom once every year. Francis said he would go look for it if I stayed here. I agreed and he went out to the forest, looking for the ones he had planted.

I stayed inside with Carmen and sat on the yellow armchair next to her bed. I fumbled to put on the bracelet she normally wore. I tied it around her waist and bent down, kissing her hand.

"Please be okay," I whispered as I moved to kiss her face. "I'm begging you,"

I wiped them away, saving them for later. I kissed her forehead and her eyes twitched. I moved to her cheek and then her fingers moved slightly. Was I seeing things or was she okay.

"Felix! Felix!" Francis yelled from down the hall. "I have the stuff!" He sped into the room, holding out the bag of herbs he held in his hand.

"That's great!" I stood up, releasing my hand from Carmen's cold, frozen-in-place hand.

"Can you mix it in quickly? I need to check her." Francis instructed and I nodded, walking over to the desk.

I grabbed the herbs out of the bag carefully and placed them in the glass container the elixir had been sitting in. We had to make this *fast*. The elixir has been sitting out for almost 5 hours, and after 4 the effects can start to wear down.

I threw the herbs into the mortar and pestle, grinding them together lightly. After they got pretty mushed, I added them to the elixir, put the lid on, and shook it hard.

I looked over at Francis—who was checking her pulse—and smiled hopefully, showing my teeth when he smiled back.

"She'll be okay, Felix." He paused, "This will work." He assured me after a couple of minutes of shaking, which was my cue to stop shaking and give it to him.

I handed the jar to him and watched my hands shake. I haven't had a feeling like this in years. I watched him feed some of the elixir into an empty IV bag, hanging it from the pole and hooking her IV to it. I watched as her eyes twitched a little as her body took in the new, stronger elixir.

"I'll give you some alone time as she wakes up. Don't try to make her alarmed." Francis patted my back and sped out of the room, hanging his stethoscope up and throwing his gloves away.

I kneeled down by the bed and held her hand, watching and feeling her fingers twitch in mine, the elixir feeding into her veins and to her heart.

After a while, the twitching stopped and I grew worried, placing my other arm on her chest softly, and placing my head in the crook of my arm.

"Please be okay… Please be okay, love," I begged, tears *falling from my eyes* for the first time since the 1700s.

The salty liquid filled my eyes, causing me to shut them tightly as my body began to shiver, my hand clenching hers tightly, kissing her soft, pale skin and whispering begs for her to be okay.

The clear water streamed down my face, shocking me as I felt it land on my arm, making a small puddle of water on my slightly tan skin.

Waterfalls formed in the pits of my deep hazel eyes and sobs were coming from my body as I shivered in pain. It had been five minutes now since Francis first fed her the elixir. I continued weeping as I pictured a clock in my mind, counting down for another two minutes. If she didn't wake up then, I would give her more of the elixir.

I squeezed her hand as tight as possible when the timer struck zero. Francis had promised this would work. Did I do it wrong? Was this my fault?

I moved my head off of her shirt and looked at the lake of salty water I had made, wiping the tears from my eyes and going to her IV. I put a full pint of the elixir into the bag and knelt back down beside her.

"Please, please love. Wake up. I don't know what to do without you." I kissed her hand as I set my head back down as I had just seconds ago.

I sat there for another five minutes, knowing when the bag was empty when I saw a visual of the empty bag in my mind. Was Carmen not going to be okay after all? I sobbed out *'please',* and *'Carmen'* and occasionally hummed parts of her song every now and then.

I stopped humming when I felt a weak hand move to my hair. "Felix?..." A tired, and weak voice asked as the hand grabbed my hair tightly.

My head shot up, "Carmen?" I looked up, only able to see a beautiful blob of colors in front of me due to the tears in my eyes. "Carmen!" I yelled, blinking the tears away and wrapping her into a tight hug. A little *too* tight.

"Felix..." she spoke exhaustingly, making me release my grasp a little bit. "What happened? One minute I was... In the pavilion with you...

And the next moment I was falling… Replaying all the memories I've ever had…" She spoke slowly and hurt, obviously tired and confused.

"Your body couldn't deal with the elixir anymore. It's old, outdated, and not fit for bodies in 2023." I explained, on the verge of tears as she pulled me into a big hug.

"I-I'm so sorry, Felix. I didn't mean to hurt you." She cried into my shirt as I cried into hers.

"You didn't, my love. It's alright. I was just worried."

I sobbed as the salty tears fell from my eyes and settled into the cotton shirt she was now wearing as I had manifested her out of her previous outfit—and into that *Queen* shirt of mine she loved so much—last night.

We cried in each other's arms for a while, and then Francis walked in. He tried to be quiet but his small shuffling sounds alerted our ears.

"Sorry. You guys can continue what you were doing, it's okay." He said as he tried to leave.

"No," Carmen coughed, "I want to leave here as soon as possible so can we talk about what happened?"

"Yes, of course." He walked over to us and told Carmen what had happened.

Twenty-Three

"You can't attend college. Not this year." Francis explained after telling me what had happened.

I told him about what happened with Jaxon and he said that he looked at his files and apparently he's going to college this year too. Francis is making us stay back because he doesn't want what happened to happen again, and neither does Felix, of course, so he said no, too.

"It's for the best, Carmen," Felix told me.

"We don't ever have to go… We know everything." I looked up at him, wondering why they were both acting like this was terrible.

"I thought you wanted to go."

"Yeah- Until I became immortal. I can touch the cover of a textbook and know everything about it in seconds and answers come to my mind instantly. Why would we need to go to school, then." It wasn't a question. I was set on the fact of not going to college if I was immortal.

"So you don't want to go at all?" Francis asked, his eyebrows furrowed. I nodded my head and he looked at Felix, nodding his head at him.

"Alright." He paused and sucked air through his teeth, "We can move back to Haines."

"No!" I protested, "I want to stay in a house in Fairbanks with you. It's… nice. You said so yourself."

"So, you want to stay in Fairbanks and then just come here when we need to?" He asked and I nodded, "Alright then. It's settled. We're gonna stay in Fairbanks."

Felix looked up at Francis. They must have been having a conversation telepathically because they were sharing something that I didn't know about.

"Alright, well, I suppose you two can go home." Francis paused, looking at Felix as he nodded his head.

"I'll be right back, love." Felix smiled as he followed Francis across the room.

I sat up on the bed and looked over at Francis' desk. Papers, pens, books, flowers, and herbs spread everywhere. There was also an empty blood bag that I assumed was mine.

I started thinking about what scenes me and Felix had seen before all of this happened, and blushed brightly to myself, remembering how those scenes looked and felt.

Francis and Felix walked in a little after, looking calm yet worried at the same time.

"You ready?" Felix asked, nodding to the door. I got up and took his hand, walking out the door in front of him.

Francis walked us out to our car and told us if anything else like that was happening then he'd make us move back to Haines.

Felix opened my door for me and sped around to the other side, starting the car almost immediately and backing out of the drive.

"Why are we driving?"

"We're going to your parent's house so they know you're okay. They were upset that I didn't take you to a hospital and that they couldn't see you."

"Is that what you and Francis were talking about?" I asked, sucking my teeth and letting go of his hand as he set it on my upper thigh instead.

"Yes and no," He rubbed his hand over my thigh, messing with the edge of the shorts I wore.

"Then what else were you talking about?"

"It's not important, darling. I promise."

"Okay," I replied, sensing he was uncomfortable and not wanting to push him to reveal anything. He looked over at me and smiled lightly, trying to prove me wrong.

We pulled up to my parent's house and Felix walked out, opening my door when he walked to my side. My parents were looking out the window. Obviously, they got my text.

I walked Felix to the door, walked in, and was met with a hug from Mom instantly. When she hugged me I got pulled away from reality, looking at *her* memories. Was this temporary elixir *that* good?

"Oh, I'm so glad you're okay!" Mom hugged me again, holding me by my shoulders. Seeing her memories hurt me. Her most prominent memory was when her mother died, which makes sense, but still hurts to see.

"Yeah… Mom." I replied, pulling away from her just to be wrapped in the strong arms of Dad.

"I'm glad you're okay," He said, pulling away faster than Mom had. His memory was of me, and the first time he met Felix. Which I thought was strange, but fitting with the text he sent to Felix before the elixir was even in Felix and Francis's minds.

"Thanks," I replied, not knowing what else to say.

I looked up and Felix—who must have been reading my mind as I saw the memories—whose eyes were wider than normal, worrying about something.

"You okay?" I asked, and he nodded, sending me a telepathic rose and closing his eyes as he shook his head.

Mom and Dad invited us in, offering coffee but we both declined, taking the cookies she had set out on the table instead.

"What exactly happened?" Mom asked, taking a sip of her warm, steamy coffee.

"Her body hasn't been getting enough Vitamin D, nor enough iron intake, so she passed out, her heart trying to live on low supplies of both, and the fact that her BPM is lower than most people, so if she passes out her heart can't speed up fast enough to help," Felix explained calmly, my hand clutching his tightly.

"Can we fix that?" Dad asked, still not saying sorry for his text, but now treating Felix like a doctor.

"No. The best that I can do is bring her outside more, but since we live in a private forest, it'll work out fine."

"Wait..." Mom began, her *thinking face* being very noticeable. "Why *were* you guys in Haines? Fairbanks is a 12 hour drive away, how did you... *Why* did you come back?"

"Carmen forgot something at my house, so we came back. We took a flight so it didn't take as long." He tried lying but my mom didn't believe him.

"No. That's not it. I can tell by how you squeezed Carmen's hand tighter." And *that*—ladies, gentlemen, and anyone else—is why it sucks that my mom is a therapist.

"I assure you ma'am, that *is* the story." Felix lied again, this time releasing his grasp on my hand a little bit.

"Sure…" Mom looked irritated like she *knew* that Felix was lying. "Whatever. The important part is that you're *okay*."

"Yeah," I replied, looking at Felix's hand, which was now basically just laying in mine. I squeezed his hand, jerking his mind and 'waking him up'.

Mom kept asking questions about what happened, what led to it, how Felix and Francis dealt with it, etcetera.

"I think we should get going if we want a chance to catch our flight," Felix explained and Mom raised an eyebrow.

"When did you get tickets? The Haines to Fairbanks flights have been booked since yesterday for the summer."

"Francis has a jet of his own we take." He lied again, although, If Francis wanted to, he *could* get a private flight.

"Uh huh…" She said, not believing him at all.

That was the breaking point. Mom had not believed Felix for the entirety of the three years we'd been together. This was it. I was not going to let her disrespect Felix again without saying anything.

"Mom!" I yelled, closing my eyes and exhaling hard after. "Can you just believe him?!" I raised my tone but tried to stay calm. "Like come on! He is telling the *truth*. What more do you need?!" I failed to stay calm as I stood up, grabbed Felix's hand, and walked to the front door.

"Honey, please." She said, following us to the door.

"No, mom. I'm done with this. I'm not going to let you not believe Felix just because you think he's bad for me!" I protested, opening the front door.

"Why do you think I hate him?" She asked, sounding offended. Almost as if *she* was the victim here.

"Ever since the first date Felix and I had you've suggested I get with someone else. But I love him, Mom. I really do."

She opened her mouth and tried to speak but I cut her off.

"No. You are *not* the victim here. If you want me to come back and see you guys ever again, tell Felix you're sorry. Tell *me* that you're sorry. Otherwise, Felix and I are going to walk out this door right now and drive away. Getting on Francis's *private jet*, and going back to *our* house." I said, trying to back Felix up on that last sentence.

"Fine. I'm sorry, Felix. You just seem so mature compared to Carmen and I guess I've just held that against you." She paused, awaiting the reaction I never gave. "And I'm sorry, Carmen. I should've supported you for the entirety of your relationship and not held a grudge against Felix. If you'd like to leave now that's fine. Please just come visit soon." She said, her voice cracking as I walked out the door.

"Thanks, Mrs. Brooks," Felix said as he walked away, looking at me with furrowed eyebrows when I let go of his hand.

"Don't accept her apology," I mumbled, getting into the car. Felix got in the driver's side and tried to grab my hand but I pulled it away, looking at my parent's house.

"I love you!" Mom called out and I exhaled hard through my nose.

"My love, what's wrong?" Felix asked, pulling off of the curb and driving away.

"Don't accept her apology," I repeated, looking down at Felix's hand, placed on the gear shifter. "I didn't mean to get upset at you, I'm sorry." I placed my hand on his but he moved it off of the gear shifter, looking at me sadly.

"Why can't I?"

He asked, his hazel eyes staring deeply at me. Almost as if he was looking for a *true* reason, buried in my brain.

"She has been rude to you ever since we started dating. It isn't fair." I put my hand back in my lap, looking down at my fingers that were now paint free, but growing fast.

"I don't hold grudges, I guess."

He shrugged, placing his cold hand on my inner thigh and rubbing his thumb over my pale skin.

He focused on the road, and after a while, he closed his eyes and manifested us at home, in the car, in our driveway.

"Hungry?" He asked as he got out of the car, speeding around to open my door, still being amazing and loving even after what had happened.

"Not really, no." I lied, my stomach growling loudly, ruining the lie.

"I'll make you something."

He said, holding my hand as I got out of the car. We walked to the house and into the kitchen, Felix placing me on one of the yellow bar stools.

He made some eggs and popped some waffles into the toaster, getting out some Nutella, *salt, pepper,* chocolate milk mix, and a butter knife.

"Do you think we could move our house to Haines?" I asked, fidgeting with my bracelet.

"I was going to talk to you about that, actually," Felix said, setting down the glass of chocolate milk and then the eggs. "I talked to Francis and he said that he is willing to move to

Fairbanks. At least until we *know* that you're okay."

"*He's* going to move to *Fairbanks*?" I asked, worried if that would draw more attention to us and The White's.

"Yeah," He said, grabbing the waffles out of the toaster and spreading Nutella on them. "There are ways to move houses and such to places, you just have to have a place to *put* them." He explained, sliding the waffles on the golden plate towards me.

"Where would he put his big ass house?" I chuckled.

"Well... I was thinking that he could use some of our forest. *Just* because we have so much extra land we're never gonna use, and he needs a more hidden place." He leaned against the counter, looking out the window at the setting sun.

"I don't really have a problem with that," I said, taking a bite of my waffles.

"Alright, I'll text him, then."

He smiled, walking up to the big windows in the living room, his hands behind his back, looking quietly at the pink, red, orange, and yellow sunset.

I finished my food and walked up behind him after I set my plate in the sink. I wrapped my arms around him, hooking our arms together, and resting my head on his shoulder as I stood on my tippy-toes.

"I love you," I said, turning my head to kiss his cheek. He smiled and turned around, unhooking our arms and instead, wrapping his around my waist, his forehead on mine.

"I love *you*, Carmen Brooks."

He leaned in and so did I, and suddenly, we were in our room, surrounded by the old paintings—along with new ones—giant, amazing plants, our large, royal bed, and a mirror that showed the amazing scene.

He pushed me onto the bed, not letting go of me or my lips.

Twenty-Four

"Felix?" I said, looking for him and walking throughout the house. "Felix?" I walked into the kitchen and saw a letter directed to Felix on the counter.

I walked up to it and grasped it in my hands, starting to take off the stamp that was placed neatly over the fold of the envelope when suddenly, a low morning voice spoke.

"Please don't open that, love." He appeared out of nowhere and wrapped his arms around me as I jumped in fright.

"Jesus- You scared me-" I said, totally not paying attention to the *morning voice* he had—which to tell you, sounded *amazing*. Like it was out of a dream or something.

"I was waiting for you to wake up. It's from *Floyd*."

"What does *he* want?" I asked as he let go of my waist, grabbing the letter.

"I'm not exactly sure. That's why I was waiting for you." He said, opening the letter and taking out the paper. He peeled back the folds and looked at it quickly, passing it to me.

"It was sent to me since they apparently didn't know where you lived." He explained as I opened the note.

Dearest Carmen,

I hope this letter finds you. I was watching you and your thoughts and decided this would be a good reminder to give you; Us Immortal Leaders don't give second chances. So you better be making the most of this.

We saw the fact that you almost died due to your previous actions, and though we hope that doesn't happen again, you better be careful. One more slip-up like that and we'll have to revisit, and you know what we mean by that.

I hope you enjoy the necklace,

Warmest Regards,

Floyd Winters.

"*'Warmest Regards'*?" I looked up at Felix after I read it.

He walked up to me and took the note from me. He scanned over it quickly and then passed it back.

"He just threatened to kill me and then says *'Warmest Regards'* as if *that* makes up for it?" I set it on the counter and picked up the envelope with a small, purple, lace-tie bag inside.

Inside the bag was a beautiful moonstone necklace, wrapped in a silver border with a fantastic chain with alexandrite gems in little silver flowers.

"Oh- Wow-" Was all I said, looking for the right words that never appeared.

"The necklace I gave you is better though, right?" Felix asked, pulling the chain necklace I wore that was stashed under the cloth of my shirt.

"Well, this one *is* pretty, but the promise ring necklace is special and important. So yes, yours is better, *Mr. Jealous*." He chuckled and grabbed the necklace from me, placing it on the counter.

"I'm Mr. Jealous, huh?" He smiled, turning me around and lifting me up. "Well, then I guess you won't care if I go hang out with Jenny and Michael alone today like we were supposed to, I suppose. Or are you *Mrs.* Jealous?" He asked playfully.

"When did we make plans with Jenny and Michael?" I asked, still stuck on *"Mrs.* Jealous*"*, too.

"It's Jenny's birthday today… Don't tell me you forgot, love." He said, setting me down on the counter and groaning as I didn't respond to the fact that I'd forgotten it was my best friend's *birthday.*

"Oh shit…"I got off the counter and walked to our room.

I opened our closet and walked inside, going through a little box I had on the top shelf labeled 'BIRTHDAY'. Felix followed but I closed the closet door as there was birthday stuff for him inside.

"Oh come on~" He whined, leaning up against the door, trying to get in, "I don't even celebrate my birthday~" He teased, reminding me that I really didn't know his birthday because he never talked about it.

"When *is* your birthday?"

I asked but instantly regretted it when he stayed quiet. I opened the door and hugged him, startling him but getting hugged back.

"I'm sorry," I said as I heard sniffles from him. "Felix... I'm sorry, I- I didn't know." I blinked away the tears that came as I felt Felix's tears hit my shoulder.

"It's okay, love, really." He sniffled, but I didn't believe him. I walked us back a bit and he sat on the bed, me on his lap.

"I'm so sorry. Please don't cry." I said as I buried my head in the crook of his neck, my hand going to his hair as I smoothed it out, trying to comfort him as much as possible.

"It's okay... I've just never talked to anyone about it."

He sniffled loudly and then wrapped his arms around me tighter, grabbing onto my shoulder blades and pushing his head into my neck.

After sitting like that with him for a while, I finally spoke up. "I'm willing to listen if you want," I suggested.

"Maybe another day. Right now we need to get ready to leave in… ten minutes." He took his head out of my neck and looked at me with his tear-stained cheeks and puffy, red eyes.

"Oh, baby~" I cooed, pulling him back to me and being satisfied when he was perfectly fine with my actions as now.

"I love you, but we gotta go if we want to make it there. We have to act as if we were still in Haines and never came home." He said, leaving a soft kiss on my neck as I nodded.

"Okay." I let go of him but missed the feeling of our hot energy touching. That wave of sensation left my body, making me feel cold and clingy.

I got up off his lap and walked back to the closet, this time taking out the birthday bin, and setting it on the bed, right next to Felix.

"What exactly is in there for me?" He smiled and wiped his tears away, looking at his wet hand for a second.

"Stuff," I teased, watching him analyze the tears that came from his eyes that were now on his hand *and* face.

"I'm sorry…" He said, looking up at me slowly.

"What for?"

I asked, turning around and grabbing out a small purple dress that Jenny had gifted me for my birthday two years ago.

"All of it I guess…" He responded, making me turn around and move the box away from him.

I sat myself down by him, wanting to hear his explanation. This was the first time in our relationship that Felix had shared his emotions with me.

Normally, he thought that because he's an immortal he doesn't have to share his emotions since he's held them for this long, but I've always tried to tell him that I'll listen, which I guess that's happening now, a lot later than I expected.

"I-" He began, coughing a little as his voice came out hoarse. "You know I'm not good at this kind of stuff, Carmen." He said, looking down at his hands.

"It's okay. I'm here. I'll listen to anything you want to tell me. Who cares if we're late? This is more important."

I said, my words just ringing in my ears. Did what I say prove what Jenny, Harley, Michael, and Alex said about me? That I spent more time caring for Felix than I did them?

"I don't mean to cry this much, I'm sorry." He said, looking up at me when I took his hand in mine, rubbing his lightly tanned skin with my thumb, trying to soothe him.

"Cry all you need, my love. I'm here for you. Sharing emotions isn't as hard as you think it is, I promise you that." I put my head on his shoulder and looked at the clock—6 minutes.

"Can we talk about this after the party? I don't want to make us late." He asked, blinking to push the tears away.

"Of course, we can," I said, smiling at him.

He pushed me back on the bed and climbed over me, his lips skimming over my lips, jaw, and neck, desperately trying to latch onto the feeling of being okay. He stopped and leaned our foreheads together, which made just enough time for me to smash my lips onto his neck.

I pulled him closer to me, my lips pressing over his defined jawline, his flushed cheeks, and his sharp neck, dropping a kiss down on his tan skin every couple of seconds. I moved myself over him and he groaned, not expecting the harshness of my force.

He lay rigidly, his spine straight and secure, stiff and tight, like he was bracing for more.

He tried to stop, but both of our minds and bodies wouldn't let us. We were both overwhelmed by the feelings we had. We weren't going to let go. Not now. Not when we are so tight in each other's arms like if we were falling off of a cliff.

Even at the thought of the cliffs in my mind, I didn't stop. Even with the thoughts of Felix dying again, I moved with him when he sat up against the headboard.

Even with the rigidness of Felix and his body, I wrapped my legs around his waist, my thighs pressing into his hips. It was those thoughts that had me wrapping my arms tightly around his neck, pressing my lips as tight as possible against his. He pushed his lips back, both of us desperate for more.

All I *could* think was *"more"*. All I could think was *"Keep going, please"*. That's it. That's all my thoughts were and all my thoughts would ever be in this moment.

Felix must have been thinking the same thing because it *did* turn into more, but not as much as I'd wished... Or that we had time for.

My hands tugged at his hair as his hands went under the *Friends* shirt I was wearing when suddenly my phone went off. It was Jenny.

Felix picked up the phone and his face turned worried. "I'm so sorry- We got caught up in something… We'll be there as soon as possible. Happy Birthday, Jenny."

He hung up and groaned, placing the phone back on the bed and taking his other hand off of my waist.

"I'll go get ready," I said as I got up off his lap and walked over to the closet doors.

I walked into the closet and closed the door, changing into the purple dress that 'highlighted my hips' as Jenny had said after she gave it to me.

I sat down at my makeup desk and the closet door opened. Felix appeared, wearing a black-on-black suit, leaning against the doorway with his arms crossed.

His face was no longer red and puffy but put together and normal looking. He walked up to me, his arms resting on the top of my chair, leaning his head around to look at me and my super flushed face.

"I guess the blush step is already taken care of then, huh?" He teased as I turned back to face the mirror.

I closed my eyes and manifested my makeup—a nice, classical look with a little bit of white eyeshadow in the corner of my eyes, and a small amount of eyeliner and mascara.

"Absolutely beautiful as always," Felix said, turning my head to look up at him, staring into his deep hazel eyes and almost getting lost.

Almost.

Almost getting lost.

Wishing I could stare at him forever.

Wishing that moments like these could last forever.

Maybe it could.

Maybe we can *make* it.

Twenty-Five

"See you soon! Bye, Carmen! Bye, Felix!" Jenny called as we left her house.

"I'm glad we went to go see her," Felix admitted, reaching his hand over and holding mine tightly.

"Me too. I just wish we didn't have to lie about still being in Haines, then maybe we could come over more."

I said, mainly saying it because I was scared my dreams would come true, but also because I truly *did* miss hanging out with her and my friends every day.

Missing our weeklong sleepovers, our funny lunch conversations, staying up late just calling each other, sharing info on school and people, and much *much* more.

"Do you *want* to move to Haines?" He asked and I shook my head. "Then this is as good as it's going to get, love." He reminded and I looked down,

"What if we could convince her to…" I stopped as Felix shook his head. "Okay,"

I said and I looked over at him, his face calm and collected, his eyes screaming in sadness and pain.

"You okay, Felix?" I asked, squeezing his hand tightly.

"Yeah… I'm okay,"

"Tell me, please, love. Your feelings are important." I assured him, turning the music low so I could have a proper conversation with him.

"I-" He began, stopping and exhaling hard, closing his eyes. "I'd rather forget about it for now, please." He said and I nodded, respecting his decision but still wondering.

He turned the radio back on and drove to the forest so we could manifest home.

"Hungry?" He asked, going to the kitchen as I nodded.

"You don't have to make anything."

"I *want* to make you something, *amour.*" He cut me off and insisted, so I didn't protest anymore.

I went to the living room and turned on the jukebox, playing some pop songs but changing it to classical music when Felix groaned playfully.

"Oh! *Debussy!*" Felix said, peering his head out of the kitchen and looking at me, a big smile plastered on his face.

"Debussy? What's that?" I asked, walking over to Felix.

"Old French music composer." He answered, turning back to the stove, still smiling.

He made me some food and I sat down at the breakfast bar, eating my food happily as he put his head on his knuckles, watching me with a smile so bright it could light up a full night sky.

"This is really good. Thank you," I said, looking up at him again and instantly getting sucked into his deep hazel eyes.

He chuckled but I genuinely couldn't look away. It's like I was addicted to him or something. I stood up and grabbed Felix's hand walking to the bedroom and pushing him onto the bed.

"You okay? What's wro-" I cut him off with a harsh, passionate kiss.

He kissed back but he was obviously confused. All of his thoughts asking if I was okay, if he should keep going, or if he should intervene.

After a while of him kissing back confused, he finally *kissed* back, being desperate as well. His fists unclench and relax, settling around my waist, and pulling me closer to him.

One of his hands climbed up my back and helped him flip me over, him now hovering over top of me.

His lips were searching, his hands hungry as I arched against him, pushing our mouths closer together, wishing they could be like that forever.

I slide my hands under his shirt and he doesn't flinch like he normally does. Instead, he accepts it, making a soft noise from deep in his vocal cords, proving he was as desperate as I was.

I stroked my fingers along his smooth, lightly tanned skin, rubbing over his lean back muscles, rubbing little circles in his skin, making him laugh softly against my lips.

All the feelings that are going on in both of our brains combine—the only thing ringing in our minds is me kissing him, him kissing me, and us kissing each other.

I moved my lips up his face as he paused. I kissed his cheekbones, nose, and his eyebrows. Savoring as much of this moment as possible.

Long, slow, needy, and desperate touches of my lips to his brows, cheeks, and forehead. Over and over I kiss him and his soft skin. Tasting him. Touching him. Over and over I whisper all the things I love and admire about him.

I move my hands to the front of his body, outside of his shirt, lining his abs and V-line, placing my hands on his chest, pulling at his shirt, pulling him closer to me—if that was even possible.

And suddenly, as soon as it started, it was over. I woke up, laying in bed next to Felix… who appeared to be *sleeping*.

Mid-thought, I felt a pair of strong arms wrap around my waist, pulling me closer to a warm, shirtless figure.

"Go back to sleep~" He cooed, his morning voice deep, sexy, and still tired.

"You actually *slept*?" I asked.

"Yeah. I was so tired from last night I just fell asleep, right next to you. A little bit after, actually."

I flushed, thinking of last night, our makeout session that wouldn't have happened unless I was as desperate as I was at that moment.

"I love you," The words coming from nowhere, but being one thousand percent true.

"I love *you*." He said, repositioning himself so I was hovering over him. "*Forever.*" He assured me, rubbing my back as he smiled against my lips.

"Forever," I agreed.

Or is it forever?

Authors Note

I have so many people I would like to thank, and I'm going to thank the teachers I had this past year first;

Thanks to; Mrs. Duffney, for being a great teacher, and a fantastic leader. You were interested in this story, even when it was nothing. You gave me so many opportunities to learn and helped me grow in lots of different ways. Thank you.

Thank you; Mrs. Gearey, for being a fun, loving teacher, and bringing joy to me this year.

You made science fun, and in my past experiences, it's kind of hard to do that. Being in your class was an amazing time that I'll sure miss. Thank you.

Thanks so much to; Mr. Martin, for being an amazing teacher, who taught us math, but in a fun way. I enjoy your small talk on different problems in the world, like bullying, low confidence, etcetera. I loved our little high-fives, hugs, and checkups you did to make sure I was okay. I'm really grateful for you and your kindness. I am *super* glad to have spent this last year with you. Thank you.

And Ms. Rossum, for believing in me, hyping me up, and introducing me to The Immortals again, my favorite Fantasy/ Romance series. And for having the Twilight saga in your room, because if you didn't, I guarantee that this story would not exist. You were an amazing teacher, and I hope that everyone that had you this last year is appreciative of that and that the people who will have you in future years are too. So thank you, for helping me make this story, and helping me be reunited with what is now my favorite series on the planet.

I also can't thank Alyson Noel and Stephenie Meyer enough. They unlocked a part of me I didn't know was there. So thank you, to both of these wonderful authors, for helping me make this story without even knowing it.

Huge shoutout to Kairi, Sydney *(Sunday)*, Alainna, and Kadence, for being interested in this and listening to my long rants about it. I love you guys, you mean a lot to me. Thank you.

Will there be a second story after The Jump?: Yes, but what do *you* think is going to happen now after Floyd threatened to come back? You'll have to wait and see.

Also, a giant thank you to you, the reader. If no one has told you recently, I'm so proud of you for just sticking around, not just through my novel, but through life.

I know this world can be such a cruel, dark, and depressing place sometimes, but that's why you're so strong for waking up every day and getting through everything that comes your way. Know that your best moments are waiting for you down the line and there are so many people that are glad you're here and that you exist. This world can be messy, but it's wonderful most of the time.

It's wonderful because there are still so many places to be, people to meet, movies to see, books to read, songs to hear, surprises to witness, sunrises and sunsets that are too pretty to miss, people to fall in love with, adventures to create, lessons to learn, art to appreciate, foods to savor, and a creating of life to never forget. Be here. Stay here, with me, your friends, your teachers, your parents, your siblings. Just stay here. The world and I are so glad that you exist.

So thank you, yes you, for coming on this journey with Carmen and Felix (as long as myself).

I love you.

About The Author

Hi! I'm Freya Johnson, the young **author** who has been working her ass off to publish this novel. I've been working on the idea of this novel for the past seven months and finally started the final draft—what you're reading now—around two months ago.

I want to say a special thank you to my Mom and Dad, for supporting me and my writing journey from the beginning. I really hope you're proud of me and how far I've come, and I hope to continue to make you proud in the coming years.

Thanks to my aunts—*Choo Choo* (Denise) and Jenny— for sharing my story on Facebook when I made posts about it, for being my first two followers on my books dedicated Instagram—more info on that in a minute—and for being interested in my writing as well!

Thank you, to my family and friends, for supporting me through this journey. I hope you can continue to support me as I continue my journey as a minor who publishes books.

More about me now, I guess. I am a minor from the Midwest whose dream has been to publish a book ever since third grade. I got into fantasy—Harry Potter and such—and then moved to romance. And then, to the best genre ever made, Fantasy Romance. I found *The Immortals* By Alyson Noel when I was in fifth grade and fell in love with the thirty pages I was able to read before the school year was over.

I picked it back up in sixth grade when my English teacher—Ms. Rossum—had five of the six on her bookshelf. I read the entire series in a month and a half, not wanting to waste a minute not being in Alyson's perfect world.

After that, *Twilight* caught my eye, and I read that entire series, falling in love with the books but also the movies, reading and watching all of the movies non-stop. I've been incredibly inspired by both The Immortals and Twilight ever since, and am so happy I can share this book with you, the reader.

What I Did to Focus and Write:

★ I listened to a lot of *Harry Styles, Panic! at the Disco,* and *Bo Burnham,* while writing this story, along with LoFi music so I focused more.

★ I set times to write—whether it was an hour or seven, I set timers and made time to write when I was free—It's very important to have time to write if you think you can make a novel in a couple of months.

★ Worked on different things alongside my novel. I am currently working on this part of my author's note while I'm in school, at the end of chapter twenty-one. *Just a question; Did chapter twenty-one being from Felix's perspective make the novel better?*

★ I worked *hard*. I worked my ass off—as I said—to create what you're reading now. I shared my progress on my TikTok and Instagram, hoping someone would want to read it, and then I looked and 400 people are willing to read this novel! It's truly an amazing thing to get so much support for this novel when I'm still a minor and didn't expect more than 10 people to be interested.

Shoutout to my Mom and Dad, thank you for trusting me and my journey as a young author, and I hope this makes you proud.

Now, I don't want to drag this on forever, but I'll say it again. I'm Freya Johnson, a minor from Minnesota who has no idea where this is going to go, or who is even going to enjoy this. But I just want you to know, I love anyone who decides to buy a copy and give this novel a *chance.*

Thank you for reading this, and I hope to see you in my next novel. I love you, keep being awesome.

Find Me on Instagram and TikTok!: @ freya.thewriter
Review My Novel on Amazon!

Stay Tuned For The Second Book In The Immortality Series: The Elixir.

Short Teaser:

One

We had just figured out that I may not live if we don't get a new elixir fast enough. Francis told us it was nothing to worry about and that I can keep drinking the temporary one until then, but it still scared me. What if I was going to die before I had even lived?

"Your body may not be strong enough for all immortal abilities." Francis leaned against the counter in his workroom as Felix gripped my hand tightly.

"What if that's not the case?" I asked, pursing my lips together tightly, hoping there was good news.

"Then I can't explain it... I'm sorry, Carmen." Francis explained, fidgeting with his ring as he looked down at his hand. "I can try to make a new elixir but it'll take a while as I haven't made a new one in centuries." Felix set a hand on my shoulder and I set mine on top of his.

"I'm willing to do whatever it takes to stay alive. My body is getting weaker every day." I looked up at Felix.

"What if the new elixir doesn't work? Or you can't make it in time?" Felix asked and Francis looked up at him.

"Then she will-" Francis began but I cut him off.

"Don't answer that!" I raised my tone, my voice raspy. "Sorry... But Felix, why do you always ask for bad answers? I'm willing to do *whatever*. No matter if it doesn't work. At least we have a chance." I said with a sad, tired voice as I looked up at him, his face wide in shock at my words.

"I..." He began but cut himself off, looking down at our hands. Mine resting on top of his. "Sorry."

Read More of; The Elixir,
Freya Johnson
Coming Mid-Late 2023

Made in the USA
Monee, IL
26 May 2023

34587813R00204